Spidey Legs Lana

# Retribution

## Book 3

**Tessa LaRock**

Cover Art by: Mark Reimann

Visit "http://www.amirarockpublishing.com"

Printed in the United States of America

**Amira Rock Publishing**

Retribution is dedicated to all those adventure lovers, romance readers, and anyone who appreciates a good paranormal twist.

# Chapter 1

**Spence's** cell phone rang; and, quickly reaching into his vest pocket, he flipped it open and answered it.

"Yeah, Pop—everything go as planned?"

Spence's father peered over the edge of the precipice along with his two sons, Ray and Travis; Marty also joined them. They had just finished watching, in amazement, Lana transforming in mid-air, wrap Evan in her cocoon, then crash against the boulders lining the river. Blood had splattered the rocks below. She was limping badly as she reached the water, dropped in, and allowed the current to take her downstream.

"Yep. She has to be injured pretty bad. And, the lead I put in that boy's chest probably made a hole the size of..." he inhaled, ingesting air along with phlegm, "...Welp, let's just say, the exit wound is probably the size of a basketball." Chuckling mildly, he withdrew a pack of cigarettes from his flannel shirt pocket and pulled one out with his teeth. Producing a lighter, he lit the end and inhaled deep.

"Shoot, you should'a seen the look on that girl's face. It was priceless."

"Well, don't underestimate them," Spence stated. "Send Ray and Travis down river to track em'. And, make sure they don't get away. I'll be there shortly."

**Lana's** arachnid form smashed against the rocks along the Haim River; and, for what seemed an eternity, her mind went blank.

The sound of her raspy breaths scratched through her ears along with the rushing waters whose droplets careened along her body and tapped at her crust covered form.

Agonizingly, rising to her feet, she took a few steps and dropped into the rushing water. The water was cold and harsh, like a slap in the face. She gasped for breath as she fought the current which was taking her downstream.

Finally latching onto a downed branch that lay across the river, she wearily pulled herself out. Now, she could understand why Evan hated water so much. As an arachnid, you had no control; you were like a fishing bobber that just floated along with the current. However, unlike a fishing bobber, you would eventually drown.

As she shook the layer of water from herself, she noticed the overpowering scent of blood. It was thick, nearly suffocating; and, the beast within her quickly revived. It desired the blood which was fresh and unsullied, tantalizing and tormenting. It would be the much needed nourishment required for healing her injuries.

Lana shook at the wanton desire that was now bringing her black widow's nature fully alert. And, immediately, her eight eyes shot downward to the large cocoon that remained pressed against her pounding thorax.

Her eyes locked to the crimson stain growing within the strands of her webbing while an exhilarated hum began to rise from within her throat and her teeth escalated to a chatter. They clattered and snapped, then suddenly, without reservation, took a bite.

The taste was divine, like the sensation of a mouth-watering delicacy whose flavor bursts upon your tongue and causes you to desire more. Evan's blood was delicious and she savored every drop, craved the silky smooth liquid that was being drawn within her injured body and providing it with strength.

A muffled scream abruptly rose from inside her cocoon as Lana's prey began to struggle. The sound pricked at her ears, and briefly she withdrew her large protruding fangs. Cocking her head, she observed in mild interest. Had she forgotten to liquefy her victim, inject it with her poisonous spew to avoid this exact annoyance.

Drawing forth the venomous juices that would immediately paralyze her victim and turn its innards to a delectable mush, Lana drew back and again plunged her fangs deep into the cocoon.

**"GAH!!"** Evan, partially in his arachnid form, suddenly burst from inside the webbing. His eyes blazed red, matching the color of his skin which was covered in his own blood. Immediately, they shot in Lana's direction.

Lana looked at him strangely—the beast consuming her, confused—still savoring the taste of its prey's delicious blood and wondering how it had managed to escape her grasp. Yet, her human nature immediately realized something was wrong.

"Evan?" Her quavering voice called out through the darkness and bestial life form that was controlling her every thought and movement.

Suddenly, her clouded thoughts became clear and a gasp rose from within her. Things were terribly wrong. And, quickly transforming into her human state, she slipped to her knees and collapsed to the ground.

Evan continued to change, bring on the beast that he needed so badly to heal his severely damaged body. He struggled at each intake of air; while his lungs, heart and kidneys were now just shredded meat. The eight legs, along with blood and tissue, easily spilled from his back. He would die if he didn't do something soon. Dropping to his hands and knees, he allowed the beast to slowly work at changing him. And, though his vision was blurred, he fought to keep Lana's still body in his sights. Travis and Ray were near. Lana had to get away.

"Lana...wake...up!" The words were a choked whisper. "You...have...to...get...away. They're...coming!"

"Uggh!!" His body shook with pain as he clutched desperately to himself, ripping the skin away with his fingers in the attempt to release the beast quicker.

"God, help me!"

He could hear the two men coming—their shouts and laughter as they ran along the river's edge heading in his and Lana's direction.

His transformation was coming too slow.

"Lana, please. Wake up!" he coughed past a mouthful of blood. "Please!"

A twig snapped just a few yards away. It was Travis.

"Damn, look at that!" Travis's silty voice rang with sadistic pleasure.

Slipping out from behind a large boulder, he slowly moved in the direction of where Evan and Lana were. And, grinning he removed the large net from his shoulder.

"This'll be a piece o' cake. And..." he whistled loudly. "...Ray, you'd better close your eyes, cause that little spider girl ain't got no clothes on." He chuckled. "Man, how lucky can ya' get?"

Ray appeared right behind his brother.

"Yeah right." He breathed heavily. "You're the one who hasn't had a girlfriend in awhile."

He then pointed to Evan who was slumped over, gasping for air. Dark blood pooled around his partially transformed body. "And, what about him?"

"Yeah, he looks a little rough," Travis agreed. "Kinda' like that deer I blasted the hell outta' two winters ago. Ya' remember that?" He laughed. "Man, that buck was a nasty mess." He thought for a moment. "Hey, maybe we should just hog-tie him; then, we'll have us a little fun."

Unraveling the netting, he stated, "Now, grab the other end of this net and help me get it over him."

"Should we wait for the others?" Ray asked.

"Nah. Ya' know Pop's on probation. He's probably half way across the county by now. And, Marty was supposed to head back to meet Spence who's on his way here.

So, come on. Let's get the spider-man netted up. I think that pretty little girl's callin' our names." His laugh was sinister.

**The** net was tossed and Evan struggled to break free. His partial transformation was making it nearly impossible to do anything but stay alive, the harder he fought, the more entangled he became.

The sound of his labored breaths scratched at his ears and his vision had finally failed. Frantically, he attempted to listen to the sounds around him, block out his labored intakes of air and listen for Lana and what was happening to her.

"Lana..." His voice was barely a whisper.

"Aw, listen to the poor little baby." Travis walked over and kicked Evan with his boot.

Evan groaned as he doubled over and dropped face first to the ground.

Travis placed his hands on his sunken stomach as he laughed. "Well, I think he's done."

"Yep." Ray pulled his white t-shirt up and rubbed his bulging stomach. "Now, come on. It's time to feed my hunger. I wanna' taste the little spider girl's blood and see what it's like to be a black widow."

They both stepped toward Lana, wicked

smiles lighting their faces.

**"Evan?"** Lana lowly mumbled as she opened her eyes and slowly lifted her head.

Evening was quickly coming and shadows crept eerily along the rocks and water. She immediately knew that something was dreadfully wrong. Her warped senses had hindered her mortification at her nudity; however, she was fully aware of it now and aware of the two men behind her.

Her entire body quaked as she frantically tried to cover herself with her hands. It was useless. She decided to concentrate on the mark on her stomach and the strands of her webbing that came from it, get it to wrap around her exposed parts she desperately needed to cover.

Slowly the silky strands poured from the spigots of her spinnerets and partially layered her skin. At least her vital parts were covered. It would have to do.

Sitting up, she wearily turned to face the two large figures that were shadowing her back.

"Well, hello, little spider girl." Travis bent and fingered a strand of her hair. "You sure are pretty."

Her voice trembled, "What do you want?"

Ray knelt down beside her; his face just inches from hers. Stale beer and cigarettes coated his heated breath and Lana immediately felt sick. Suddenly, he grabbed her by the arm.

"Look how skinny you are. You're too damn skinny. Skinny people make me sick—except for my brother, of course." He grinned over at Travis and pointed a thick finger in Evan's direction. "Well, that's what good being skinny will do ya'. See your boyfriend over there—well, he's about done because he ain't got no guts."

Ray quickly turned to his brother, a malicious twinkle in his eyes. "Ya' get it, Travis!" He laughed. "No guts!" Slapping a heavy knee, he stood while pulling Lana up to him.

"No!" She suddenly felt faint as her head spun and her knees grew weak. "Evan!"

"Come here!" Ray grabbed her head and pulled it against his weighted chest. He smelled of sweat and cheap cologne. "I can't stand all that screeching; so, you need to shut your mouth."

"Hey," Travis asked, "how 'bout we bound and gag her? Maybe tie her to a tree?"

"Sure...," Ray agreed.

"Evan!" Tears streamed Lana's cheeks as she fought to get away. Ray tightened his grip and lifted her from the ground.

"No! Let me go! Let me go!" Suddenly, her foot caught him in the groin.

The blow sent Ray doubling over in pain. "Gah! You little..." he gasped for a breath.

"Travis—get her!" Irritation flared upon his angry face. "She's gonna' pay for that!"

Lana spun in the attempt to escape; however, Travis's lanky form was immediately behind her. Grabbing her by the arm, he shoved her face first to the ground. Then, placing a sharp, boney knee to her spine, he quickly pulled a rope from his back pocket and bound her hands and feet.

"What about her transforming into that

beast?" Travis hurriedly asked. "She'll definitely break through the ropes."

"If she does, we'll just shoot her."

Ray stepped toward her and bent to look into her terrified eyes. "I'm almost certain her boyfriend's dead. So, that means that she can die too. Right, little girl?"

Evan's dead? No, he can't be! Turning her head, Lana stared blindly at his body.

"Evan...

"He's not gonna help you," Ray sneered.

He and Travis then lifted her to her feet and dragged her toward a large oak tree which stood just feet away from the river's edge.

The idea of Evan being gone made her numb, lifeless to the torture she would soon undergo. And, if Evan was dead, it really didn't matter what they did to her. She now knew that she couldn't survive without him—didn't want to survive without him.

Her tears ran like the river that was just feet away and she could feel the arachnid wanting to come to being.

Stop crying! She angrily shouted inside. Just stop it!

She thought of transforming; however, with Evan's blood being so potent, she may not be able to stop the beast from preying on him if he was still alive. No, she shook her head; she couldn't transform. Evan would not only be in danger from these two men, but also from her.

Lana's head felt as if it were full of sludge, thick with a substance that made it nearly impossible to think. She didn't want to think. If Evan was dead, all she wanted to do was die—die along with him.

# Chapter 2

**The** ropes tore at Lana's wrists and ankles; and, the bark of the tree scraped at her front as she was pushed face first against it.

"Hey," Travis suggested, "let's tie her crucifix style, like they did Jesus." Pulling her arm taunt, he stretched it toward a low branch. "Then, if she misbehaves, we can whip her with a switch." A heinous laugh tore from his lips.

Ray, laying down the rifle, secured her other arm to another branch which was just slightly higher. "That might hurt." He placed his hand to his stomach as a sardonic look crossed his face. "But, I do owe her for driving my boys into my gut."

As the two men's conversation continued, Lana cringed and her body shook. Her teeth chattered; and, she bit her lip in the attempt to make them stop. Tears streamed her puffed and scraped cheeks. Involuntarily, she began to sob.

Travis finished tying her arm and hurriedly searched the area looking for the perfect stick to fashion into a switch. Finding one, he quickly removed the smaller, useless branches, snapping each one off as he walked back to where his brother and Lana were. The stick cut through the air as he eagerly whipped it to and fro like a child with a new toy.

Lana's head began to spin.

The sound of the thrashing whip and fervent beating of her captor's over-eager hearts made her sick. Closing her eyes, she strived to listen to anything else—anything that would take her mind off the torture that was to come. Her stomach roiled and she suddenly felt nauseous.

"Are you ready for this?" Ray whispered into her ear as he pressed his large body against hers. "Next time you won't fight back."

"No! Please!" Lana's heart banged against her ribs as his body pressed tighter. Then, he was gone. A moment passed and Lana slowly opened her eyes. Suddenly, the switch snapped against her skin.

"Oh, my god!" Her body bucked against the pain and her knees buckled beneath her. Turning her head, she gasped for air.

**Evan** opened his eyes. "Lana?" Her cries tore through his ears and he forced himself to his hands and knees.

"Leave her alone," he gasped.

Travis quickly spun. "Hey, look who's still alive." He lowly chuckled as he sauntered in Evan's direction. Planting his feet and grinning maliciously, he swung the stick. The switch, hurriedly responding to his thrashing arm, bowed and snapped. It cracked Evan over and over.

"Man, you spiders are tough," Travis stated.

"No! Stop!" Lana cried.

Travis's gaze briefly cut to her; and, without

missing a beat, he remarked, "Oh, don't worry, I'll stop when it's your turn."

"Lana..." Evan whispered. Curling himself into a ball, he took the brunt of the blows to his back. He'd prefer it was him taking the beating than her. He would endure it as long as he could or until he was killed from loss of blood.

Tears wet Lana's cheeks and she closed her eyes. The sound of the whip, snapping at Evan's skin, was unbearable.

Ray stood behind her laughing as Travis's arm suddenly dropped to his side. He was panting.

"Man, am I gettin' a workout today." He rubbed a hand across his sweated forehead. "How about you take over here, brother; and, let me go back to the girl. I'd rather be sweatin' while doin' something else besides beating this freak to a pulp."

Ray responded, "Nah, it's too hot..."

"All right then." Travis turned back to Evan and the whip lashed again at Evan's already battered skin.

"No!" Lana cried. Biting at her lower lip, she attempted to keep her black widow form at bay. However, the arachnid was too strong and she could no longer keep it under control, Evan's beating was horrible. It had to stop.

The beast, screeching in rage, suddenly overtook her body, and burst from her skin. "No," she panted against its coming as the eight legs readily tore from her back and she was rapidly transformed.

"Shit!" Ray shrieked. Immediately, twisting on his heels, he headed for the rifle. Curse after curse spewed from his shaking lips as sweat broke upon his body and he stumbled toward where the gun lay.

Lana quickly spun; and, snatching up his heavy-set body, she effortlessly slammed him to the ground. Within seconds, her large mass was upon him, swiftly wrapping him in her webbing.

Ray screamed in terror, blubbering for her to stop; however, the beast had been unleashed. Its teeth chattered and the venom it used to paralyze its prey readily poured into its jutting fangs. Quickly, they plunged into his thick waist.

"Travis!" Ray screamed. "Get her off me! Get her off!" The webbing was quickly encasing his body, covering him from head to toe. Moments passed as he kicked and struggled then, suddenly, became still.

"Oh, my god!" Travis's frozen feet suddenly plowed forward and he was hurriedly heading in the direction of the rifle. His hands shook as he grabbed the gun, turned, and took aim.

Lana's eyes flared red and cut in Travis's direction as a bullet ripped from the barrel and tore into her chest. Dropping Ray's dead body, she charged.

"Shit! Shit! Shit!" Travis fumbled in his pocket for another bullet; however, within seconds, Lana covered the space between them and, immediately, had him secured within her legs.

"No!" he screamed as he turned the rifle on her. Within seconds, the weapon was whipped from his hand and bent into a "U".

Lana watched him—watched and listened as he screamed and kicked, thrashed about in the attempts to get away. Webbing shot from the hourglass-shaped marking upon her thorax and wrapped its way around him completely to his neck.  His shrill voice was becoming a nuisance, making her irate.

Lana's immense fangs slipped from her open mouth, ready to consume of his bodily fluids and fill her unquenchable thirst. However, a familiar scent suddenly rustled through the many tiny hairs covering her body. Quickly, she dropped Travis and spun.

Travis grunted once and his skull popped as she scurried across him in Evan's direction.


**Spence's** arachnid senses immediately picked up the scent of blood and he quickened his steps. Booger was to his left, keeping pace, while Marty followed quite a few yards behind.

Marty called out to them, "Hey, Spence... Booger... wait up. I can't keep up with you guys."

Spence's gaze cut to Booger who was quickly surpassing him. He knew that it was the smell of fresh blood that was driving his friend forward.

"You smell it too, huh?" he asked.

Booger only nodded. His stomach was twisting in knots at the hunger pangs that came with his now being a newborn arachnid and needing to feed. Easily scaling the rocks and boulders, he passed Spence and was several yards ahead now.

"Don't touch the girl; she's mine," Spence shouted to him as Booger raced ahead and disappeared into a clump of trees. "If you do, I'll have'ta kill ya'."

Booger ignored him, the scent now pulling him in like a magnet. Breaking through the last group of trees, he abruptly froze in his tracks.

Ray's body lay just feet away. His features were sullen and drawn, almost blue. The scent of another arachnid beast emanated from his flesh while his blood had been defiled by the poison that only an arachnid possesses. He also saw Evan lying a few yards away in the clearing. Blood lay in a large puddle around him. Then, his gaze shot to Travis, who was completely wrapped, except for a bloodied stump.

Booger had stumbled upon a smorgasbord. However, a series of alarms went off in his head with the knowledge that the poison in Ray's system was from that of a black widow female. The desire for the female was strong and his lower extremities readily knotted. However, his hunger needed to be fed; it was driving him crazy. The female could wait until he was at full strength and able to force her to submit.

So, allowing the beast to consume him, Booger slowly began to transform. It came little by little and was more painful than when he had transformed for Spence at the trailer. Spence's old man and brothers had laughed and scoffed at his transformation, said he had screamed like a girl. They had always mocked him, called him dummy when he stuttered. Well, they certainly weren't laughing now, he thought. And, they would have absolutely nothing to say as he drank of their bodily fluids and drained them dry. He liked Spence most of the time; however, Spence's brothers deserved to die.

Booger's chuckle was heinous as his body finally completed its metamorphosis and he charged in Travis's direction. Travis would be first; he was already wrapped and his brain matter was extremely potent.

Just as Booger finished his maddening feeding frenzy, Spence rounded the corner and appeared through the trees.

Spence's eyes were burning with fury as he stared at the carnage before him.

"What the hell did you do to Travis and Ray, Booger? And, where is the girl?"

Rage edged Spence's shoulders and his body immediately began to transform.

**Lana** sat within the branches of a tree watching the scene below. Curiously, she observed, while in her arachnid form, Booger who had transformed and was feasting on Travis. Now, she watched as Spence entered the area and also took on his beastly form. Evan lay just below her; she could hear him lowly moaning.

"Evan..." Her human senses gradually began to focus and the images of what she had just done to Ray and Travis seeped upon her mind. Oh god! What did I do? I've become a monster!" She wanted to cry, to scream, tear away at the abomination that was encasing her human body. What she now was made her sick, made her hate what she had become.

If I can just get Evan to safety, I'll never transform again. She thought. Never! However, for now, she would have to remain in her black widow form, use the creature to get Evan away where he could take time to mend. With two arachnid males present, she was unsure of how she could reach him and escape without a confrontation.

It didn't matter. She just knew she had to get to him so they could make their escape.

# Chapter 3

**"I'll** kill you, Booger!" Spence's form had grown larger, stronger; he had become a colossal-sized arachnid while Booger was much smaller—a Schnauzer compared to a Great Dane.

Booger looked upon Spence as another beast coming to feed—feed upon the two who lay in the open, and claim the female arachnid that was sitting in a tree overhead. However, his newborn tendencies would never allow another to claim his quarry or the female who smelled so delicious, nearly as delicious as the bath of blood that was covering the entire area and filling his miniscule nostrils. Dropping Travis's lifeless body, Booger shifted and charged at Spence.

**The** two beasts collided, like two freight trains hitting head-on. Their fighting pushed them closer and closer to the water and their shrieks and screeches resounded off the trees and rushed throughout the forest. All wildlife within the vicinity remained quiet, still as possible as each creature cowered and feared for its life.

Lana hurriedly made her move while Spence and Booger were fighting. Making Evan her target, she shot webbing in every direction, every place but where she wanted it to go. She needed to focus, concentrate on controlling the strands. It shot from her spinnerets, from high in the trees and curled around a tree branch lying several feet from where Evan was.

She would have to try again.

Her eight marble-like eyes flashed as the threads streamed from her body, and catching a slight breeze, drifted and entangled themselves within the netting surrounding Evan. It had been pure luck.

Quickly, she went to work encasing his body. And, drawing him tightly within her cocoon, Lana yanked him into the air.

Evan screamed in pain as the strands were tearing into his injuries, causing the slowly healing wounds to reopen. Lana attempted to control her webbing and pull him to her. It was taking too long and he was making too much noise. The ruckus drew Booger's attention.

Foolishly turning away from Spence and the fight, Booger watched as his prey was being taken; drawn within another arachnid's cocoon and slipping away. Suddenly, Spence grabbed him with four claw-like legs and within seconds ripped him to pieces.

The fight was over.


**Marty**, who had been hiding, instantly broke into a sweat. Horror at what he just witnessed and the loss of his friend shot blood to pump in his ears and his body to tremble in terror.

Spence ignored him and immediately turned

his attention to Lana, who he knew was just over-head.

Lana fought to keep her grip on the thick branch as Spence, who was twice her size, was up the tree within seconds and bounding upon her. However, the branch gave way, sending them both crashing to the ground.

Two of her eyes cut in Evan's direction, making certain he was still alive. He was. Quickly, scrambling to her feet, she hurried to place herself between him and Spence.

Suddenly, Spence lunged at her.

Lana reacted quickly as he slammed into her and sent her spiraling backward and barely landing upright. Quickly, she shifted her weight while waiting for the next blow.

Spence's teeth chattered loudly and his fangs were dripping with venom. Lana watched his bulging eight eyes as they blazed fiery red and cut in every direction in search of an advantage to take her out.

Suddenly, Spence was scurrying for a near-by tree and racing up its trunk. A brief moment passed as he disappeared within its heavy layer of leaves. Then, all of a sudden, he sprang from one of the limbs; his webbing was shooting in every direction.

Lana was unable to move herself and Evan quick enough. And, they immediately became entangled as Spence hurriedly worked his strands around her. Screeching in fear, she struggled to break free and fight back.

"Evan..." her human thoughts cried out, "he's

too strong. I can't beat him!"

Evan staggered to get to his feet. "Lana," His voice was barely audible. "Fight back. You have to fight back!"

Spence's webbing shot in Evan's direction, circled his body, and tossed him through the air like a broken toy. Something snapped as Evan's body hit a tree several yards away and he dropped to the ground.

"Evan?" Lana's human thoughts and emotions were fading in and out like bad reception on a radio.

"Evan, move!" she suddenly cried inside. "You have to move!" A round moment passed, seeming to be an eternity as all eight of her eyes, every hair on her body, and every sense she had remained focused on him.

"Please, move."


**Spence's** human and beastly mind relished in Lana's cries and enjoyed every attempt she made at breaking free; he had dreamt of this every night, wallowing in her struggle and the fear she would emanate.

His webbing was tight, secure; she would never escape it. And, now that he had her, the black widow female, he could do with her as he wished.

One shriek after another reverberated across the forest as he lay on top of her and slowly pressed against her. His weight was crushing, drawing every depleting breath from her lungs; and, her strength was quickly failing.

Lana watched through terrified eyes, Spence's massive dark form above her as he drove her inches into the forest floor. Evan had once explained that the size and strength of an arachnid was determined by a person's character. If a person was evil or filled with hatred, they would be larger, stronger, full of immense power—Spence was indestructible.

Yellowed venom soaked his jutting fangs. It dripped upon her and raced along the sides of the webbed cocoon where her limbs were secured. In one bite, she could be finished.

Frantically, her eight eyes searched for a means of escape, a way she could free herself and run, run as far away as fast as she could. Suddenly, she screamed. Spence's fangs were hooked in her throat. Venom pumped within her system and snaked throughout her body. It sent pain rushing to every inch of her black widow form, pain that was indescribable.

Inside her human mind, she wanted to scream, cry, break free of this nightmare that was filling her with so much pain. It made her want to vomit.

"Get off her!" She suddenly heard Evan shout. For a moment, she thought she was imagining it, thought it was the excruciating pain that was nearly driving her to insanity.

Suddenly, Spence ripped his fangs from her throat and dropped upon her like a huge stone. Evan, using a large stick, had skewered him like barbeque on a grill.

"Lana, use your eyes!" he shouted. "You have

to use your eyes!"

Spence was shaking his head, attempting to focus. His huge fangs were a hair's breadth from Lana's face. Shrieking in rage, he again sunk his fangs into her neck.

Lana began to panic.

Suddenly, Spence bucked as Evan struck again. However, this time it was with his fangs— Evan was in his arachnid form, tearing at Spence from every angle.

Using this to her advantage, Lana caught three of Spence's eyes in her gaze. The three eyes locked and the others quickly followed suit. However, it was too late. He was under her spell.

Lana was careful about what she commanded, unsure if he would listen, or turn to attack Evan.

"Back away!" her mind shouted. "Back away!"

He paused, then, slowly moved off of her.

Evan quickly tore the webbing from her with a swipe of his leg. Then, unable to remain the beast any longer because of his injuries, he dropped to his knees and gulped for air.

Lana slowly maneuvered her way to her feet, again positioning herself between Evan and Spence. She watched Spence closely, never taking her eyes from his which burned blood red, burned with hatred for her. His poison was moving rapidly throughout her body; however, her gaze remained fixed, an unbreakable padlock that had no key. Her fangs were bared, dripping with the black widow female's venom and ready to strike within a seconds notice.

Suddenly, she attacked.

Ripping Spence's thorax in two, Lana became deadly, the black widow with the power to kill. Spence's entire anatomy was open and vulnerable; and, drawing her head back, Lana then plunged her fangs deep within him.

Spence writhed and fought to break her hold as his webbing poured haphazardly from the small spigots lining his arachnid form and poison cursed throughout his body. It mixed with the blood that was beginning to curdle and thicken, and his bodily fluids were rapidly melding to a liquid clot.

Lana clung tightly to him, determined to finish him off. And, as the moments passed, his fighting came to an abrupt halt. He was finally dead.

Lana stood over Spence. Her body weaved and she was barely able to stand. And, though she had drained Spence of all his fluids, she needed to feed, replenish her strength and fight off the poison that was rapidly circulating throughout her body.

Quickly, her arachnid turned toward Evan, turned toward the scent of fresh blood that emanated from his wounds.

No! Lana fought against the beast and made it succumb to her wishes.

Then, turning back to Spence, she finished what was left.

**Marty** was hidden several yards away. His mouth snapped shut as he fought the bile sloshing in his stomach and quickly rising to his throat. His body shook violently and urine trickled along his quivering legs. Tearing his frozen feet from the ground, he began to run.

"Holy shit! Holy shit!" he breathed as he stumbled through the trees away from the river and the carnage.

Evan caught a glimpse of him. And, uncertain as to who would be next on Lana's menu, he hollered over his shoulder, "Run! Run as fast as you can!"

# Chapter 4

**Ches** sat on the couch in his living room. His shirt was off and he had stripped down to jogging shorts. Two soda cans sat on the coffee table before him; he was using them as targets for his webbing, working on controlling the strands and making them flow in the direction he wanted. He had been practicing all morning while a football game was being played on television. And, though the sound was turned way down, he could still plainly hear it. Horns blared as his team scored the winning touchdown; he didn't even notice.

"Come on, come on!" His eyes narrowed as he concentrated on the cans and webbing poured from the red bands lining his sides and lie in heaps upon the couch and floor. The strands fought for self control as they missed the cans and wrapped around his sunglasses.

"Man!" He slammed his open palm on the table.

The table immediately split in two, sending the two halves colliding and crashing to the floor.

"Holy crap!" He guiltily spun around to see if Trey was anywhere nearby watching. Unfortunately, he was.

Trey began to choke on the water he was drinking.

"Ches," he cleared his throat. "You can explain that to Aunt Liv."

Ches threw his hands in the air in innocence. "I swear, I didn't mean it."

Trey tossed the empty water bottle he was drinking from into the sink. "Well, you can tell her that while she's pulling every blonde hair outta' your fat head."

"I'll just tell her you did it."

"Yeah, like she'd believe you. She knows I'd never break anything of hers. She'd snap me in two."

"Look, I'll pay for it."

"Oh, I know you will."

"No compassion, buddy?" Ches made an attempt to put the table back together, however, failed.

"Welp, considering I told you not to get involved with that girl and you did anyway—no."

"Geez, I'll keep that in mind next time you bring home one of those crazy broads who ends up out on the lawn yelling, 'Trey, you worthless piece of crap! Get out here!' Or, this is even better." Ches mimicked a female's voice. "'Trey, oh, Trey, please come out...Please. I love you...'"

Suddenly, a wooden spatula cracked him upside the head.

"Ow!" Ches spun as his hand flew to touch the rising bump. "What the heck was that for?"

"I just think you're trying to start a fight. And, I thought I'd beat ya' to it."

Ches smiled wide. "So, ya' wanna take a shot at the beast?"

"No," Trey responded as he rushed toward the couch and dove upon Ches. "I wanna take a shot at you!"

Tumbling across the broken coffee table, they landed on the living room floor. Ches quickly grabbed Trey around the throat, and bending, he spoke into his ear, "Is this what you want, buddy?"

"No, but this is what you might get if you don't wise up," Trey breathed as he drove his knee into Ches's groin.

Ches's eyes angrily flashed crimson and he bit back the rage that was coming to the surface along with his beast. Then, quickly catching himself, he rolled to his side and painfully sucked at air, "All right, all right; I get the message."

Trey hoisted himself to an elbow. "Look, Ches, I love you, man—you're like my brother. However, all I can see is hurt in the future from all this.

Sure, you may be able to crush a softball in one hand, run like a cheetah and sail through the air like Batman; but, come on, you have to get back to the real world. We have classes startin' soon and you have to get back into the swing of things, like school and graduating.

Today is the last day to register for our classes; and, you've been sitting on the couch the whole day playing with your string. Now, it's time to get up and get with the program."

Ches looked up at his friend, the pain in his groin still searing from his navel down. Without Trey knowing, he had carefully wrapped his webbing around Trey's lower half. Then, jumping to his feet, he yanked Trey upward against the ceiling; and following suit, he too shot upward and trapped him beneath his arms and legs.

"Holy..." Trey cried out.

"And, you want me to give this up?" Ches asked.

Trey smiled. "Guess not. But, just promise me one thing. If I end up getting bit and becoming one of you guys, just don't let me eat anything gross. You know how queasy my stomach gets."

Ches quietly laughed.

Suddenly, Trey grabbed him by the head with both hands and kissed him on the cheek.

"Ew!" Ches irritably wiped a hand across his face. Immediately, he lost his grip and he and Trey slipped from the ceiling and crashed to the floor. Ches groaned as Trey landed on top of him.

"I win!" Trey shouted.

"Bull." Ches achingly sat up and shoved him to the side. "That was just dirty. Sickening if you ask me."

"Oh, you loved it." Trey chuckled. "Best kiss you ever had."

"Yeah, just like drinking toilet water." They both laughed as Ches tore the webbing from Trey and released him.

Trey's cell phone suddenly began to ring. Pulling it from his pocket, he flipped it open and answered, "Hello?" Getting up, he went to the kitchen. His mood had suddenly turned serious. He was keeping his voice to a whisper.

Ches could hear a handful of Diana's words on the other end, something about Evan this and Evan that. Just his name boiled Ches's blood. And, he certainly was in no mood to listen to Diana's annoying yammering; however, he was worried about Lana.

Cleaning up the mess in the living room, Ches then grabbed the two pieces of broken coffee table, carried them to the back door and set them outside. He would carry them to the trash later.

Then, walking back into the kitchen, he stood with his arms crossed looking at his friend.

Trey finished his conversation and flipped his cell phone closed.

"So, what was Lana doing?" Ches asked. Suddenly, he felt agitated, irate.

"I thought you could hear everything?" Trey remarked.

"I could only pick up a few words; and, some things I don't wanna' hear."

"Well, I don't know if you wanna' hear this."

"Go ahead and try me."

Trey hesitated. "Well, Lana attacked Diana right after we left."

"And..." Ches interjected.

Trey took a glass from the cupboard, filled it with water, then drank it.

"It was because Lana was biting Evan and Diana tried to stop her."

Ches's normally warm, azure-colored eyes slowly turned from red to black and his fists tightened in knots. The tension was thick, like swimming in quicksand.

Quickly turning his head, he tried to avoid Trey's insistent stare.

"I knew you'd be upset," Trey stated.

Ches's breath was strained. "We were just there. What is he doing to her; she would never harm anyone, or bite anyone, unless it was absolutely necessary." Turning, he walked into his bedroom.

"Ches—what are ya' doing?" Trey called in through the closed door. "And, what about classes? Today is the last day to sign up."

"They can wait," came a reply.

"Damn you, Ches. I have to graduate next year or my ass is toast. And, the last time I left you go alone, you ended up dead—deader than that cow they killed for those leather boots you always wear."

"Well, this is different."

A moment passed and Ches appeared at the door dressed in his camouflage pants, t-shirt and his boots. Moving quickly past Trey, he grabbed his keys from the hook by the kitchen entrance and headed toward the garage.

"Ches, leave her go."

Ches opened the garage door, then paused.

For a moment, Trey thought Ches may have changed his mind and listened to his advice.

However, without turning, Ches stated, "No. I can't do that." Then, closing the door behind him, he climbed into his jeep, and started the engine.

The rumbling of the big motor vibrated the entire house as Ches hit a button on his remote and opened the garage door. His thumb tapped at the steering wheel as if it would make the door open faster. And, before he heard the final bang of metal as it locked in place, he threw the shifter into reverse and backed out of the garage. Gunning the motor, he headed in the direction of the cabin.

Trey watched him from the living room window. "Well, I have to go sign up for classes," he spoke to the emptiness. "You go chasing after the impossible."

Then, looking toward heaven, Trey spoke to his sister.

"Tricia, what am I supposed to do? He's gonna' get hurt again." He stood for a moment in the silence; then, quietly he blew a kiss toward the ceiling and heaven in hopes it would reach her.

Registration would be over soon; he needed to get moving. Going into his bathroom, he showered and dressed, then headed toward campus.

# Chapter 5

**"Evan!!"** Lana, now in her human form, screamed his name at the realization of what she had done. Mortification, shame, and disgust were an insurmountable tidal wave pounding upon her, driving her thoughts into a whirlwind of despair.

"Oh my god!" Suddenly, she collapsed to the ground.

**When** Lana awoke, she was back at the cabin in Evan's bed. The small lantern on the nightstand was lit and the room was completely quiet. It was 3:19 pm according to the digital clock.

Through all the horrible dreams and raging tears, she had forgotten about Evan's gift which was now sitting on the nightstand. His birthday had been ruined.

Tears welled in her eyes as all her memories returned. And, pulling the quilt up over her head she began to cry. Only moments passed and the black widow within her was aching to break free.

"No!" she stated through clenched teeth as the tears fell along her face. "I won't let you come out, not ever again! Not ever!"

She was exhausted, exhausted beyond comprehension. Tiredness and fatigue overtook her and she drifted back into a restless sleep.

Four days passed as Lana fought against her flooding emotions, hating what she had become, and hating the creature that lurked within her. And, though Evan was a black widow also, he was probably repulsed by her, disgusted at her heinous act.

Her body wracked with sobs as she fought against sleep, the creature and the horrific thing she had done.

On that fourth day the bedroom door opened. Quickly, she ran the back of her hand across her tear ridden eyes and rolled onto her side to face the wall. She remained still, not wanting Evan to know she was awake.

Evan stepped quietly toward the bed. It had been nearly a week since they were attacked by Spence. Somehow, he had managed to carry Lana home.

Getting her into bed, he finally collapsed on the couch and remained there for two days as his own body slowly healed and, little by little, he regained his strength. And, though he ached to be with her, comfort her in her time of need, he knew she had to deal solely with her black widow beast. For, it had been the same for him after the first time he had killed someone—that someone being his mother.

Sitting next to her on the edge of the bed, he laid his hand on her shoulder.

"Lana, I know you're awake. I could hear you crying."

"No, I wasn't," she sniffled. "That was someone else."

He mildly chuckled. "I don't think so. I can recognize any sound you make. Remember, everything about you draws me to you, and only you."

"I don't want you to be drawn to me," she blubbered from beneath the blanket. "I'm evil, repulsive; and, I don't wanna' come out."

"Please." He gently pulled the blanket from over her face. "You need to get something to eat.

"No, I don't wanna' eat—not ever again. I'm an animal—a creature from the dark lagoon!" She disappeared beneath the blanket again.

"Well, I made some homemade chicken and dumplings; it's Grandmother Hobbs' recipe. She taught me how to make it and I think it turned out pretty good. You should try some."

"It does smell good," she mumbled. "But, I'm still not eating." She pulled the quilt down from over her eyes and looked at him. Dark circles encased each of her sockets which were red-rimmed and creased.

Evan couldn't help but touch her face. She looked tired, worn out, like there was no relief from any of her pain or burden. And, though it brought about an incurable ache, he thought he would tell her about his mother whom he killed over one hundred years ago. He thought that maybe it would help her to understand that she wasn't alone. His voice was low as he spoke.

"Lana, did I ever tell you what happened when I was first bitten and what I did to my mother?"

She thought for a moment. "No. You never did." She watched as his features became drawn and the beautiful sparkle left his eyes. He began to wring his hands as his gaze dropped to the floor.

"Well...," he began, "...when I was about seven or eight, my father had taken me to a baseball game. We used to love to go to the games." He faintly smiled as he thought about the fun they had.

Then, his smile quickly faded and he continued. "Well, that's where I was bitten, at one of the games. I was sitting in the bleachers and one of the infected black widows bit me on the back of the leg. I wasn't sure what it was.

Anyhow, my father put some salve on it and we finished watching the game; however, by the time we got home, I was really sick."

He looked up to see if she was still listening. She was.

"Anyway, my mother, who I loved more than anything, was so worried. She called the family physician to come out to the house; however, a bad storm had set in and the doctor was unable to make it. She sat up with me the entire night, until..." Evan paused as sadness shadowed his features while he could still see his mother's frightened face and feel her trembling hand against his.

His mind began running through the event again for the thousandth time, trying to figure out how he could have stopped it—what he could have done to prevent her death. But, no matter what, it had happened, and she was gone.

He had cried for days and nights—years it

seemed. At times, the memories made the pain unbearable. And, he certainly couldn't have blamed his father, whom he loved also, for chasing him away.

"Lana, I killed my mother," he hastily stated as he once again fought that pain. "I became the beast and strangled her with my webbing."

Lana's eyes were wide as saucers as she listened; she was unaware she had been holding her breath. "Oh, my god," slipped from her lips, as her hand quickly appeared from beneath the blanket and took his.

"Evan, I'm so sorry. That must have been terrible."

"Welp...," his face slightly changed as sadness held his eyes, "...for years I was scared, hated myself for what I had done and for what I had become. But, somehow, I learned to live with it. Grandmother Hobbs was a big help; she continuously reassured me each and every day that it wasn't my fault. She even told me that someday someone would find a cure—I guess she was referring to Jacob Winslow."

He frowned at the mention of Jacob's name. "She'd be mortified if she knew he had used my blood for his own benefit; but, who could blame him. When it comes to Lucinda, he would do anything."

He smiled lightly. "Well, that's what happened."

"I had no idea." Lana ran the back of her arm across her tired eyes. "I'm so sorry."

Evan stood to his feet. "You don't have to

apologize. It is what it is.

Now, come on, get dressed and come out and get something to eat. The food's getting cold."

"I am really hungry; but, I don't have any clothes."

"I've already taken care of that." He handed her a clothing bag labeled Maurice's.

"What...another set of your ex-girlfriend's clothing?"

He softly laughed. "No. I knew it upset you, so I went and did a little shopping while you were sleeping yesterday."

Apprehension shadowed Lana's weary features.

"What?" He raised a crooked brow. "You look worried. Don't you think I could pick out something nice for you? I bet I didn't tell you that I knew Marilyn Monroe and taught her everything she knew about how to dress. Well, at least when she wore dungarees..."

"The actress, Marilyn Monroe?" Lana interrupted. "You knew her?"

"Yeah, I knew her back when she was just plain old Norma Jeane and she was an orphan—kinda' like me—before Hollywood and fame messed her all up. Grandmother had introduced us. Those were her clothes you were wearing the other day."

A lump formed in Lana's throat and she swallowed hard. "You kept her clothes all this time?"

"Yeah," Evan replied. "I don't know why; I guess it's kinda' strange. I just thought that with her being famous and all..." He stopped short. "I don't know what I was thinking. I saw her in the movies several times and...well...I don't know. It was a shame she died."

"So, she was your girlfriend?"

"For a short while, until she was forced to marry or return to the orphanage she was raised at."

"You didn't love her and wanna' marry her? She was gorgeous."

"Well, I did love her; but, as far as marriage, she had no idea what I was. And, what I felt for her was nothing like what I feel for you." He looked at her and smiled his perfect smile.

Lana's cheeks turned pink.

"Now, come on," he stated, "Let's get something to eat."

"Wait..." she reached for the bag sitting on the nightstand. "I got this for you, for your birthday. I'm sorry you didn't get it."

Evan gently touched her cheek as he took the bag. "You don't need to apologize; it's not your fault. Did you win it at the game?"

She nodded her head.

"Did you cheat?" He teasingly shook a finger at her.

Lana measured an inch between her index finger and her thumb as she shrugged. "Maybe a little. But, how did you get it? And, where? It should have dropped when I transformed."

"I noticed you had it when I first saw you in the trailer park. Then, after transforming you didn't have it; so, I went back to look for it a few days ago and found it upstream aways. You're lucky it hasn't rained for nearly a week."

"Then, you know what it is?"

He remained silent for a moment, then the corner of his mouth curled upward. "Yeah, I kinda' looked inside. I'm sorry."

Lana's shoulders slumped and her lower lip jutted forward. "Now, it's not a surprise."

"Ah, yes it is." Laying the bag down, he gathered her in his arms.

"It's the best present I've ever gotten."

She glanced up at him through sad eyes. "But, you don't even know if it fits."

"Well, then, how about I try it on." Quickly releasing her, he took the bag and removed the hat from inside it. Then, placing it on his head, he smiled at her. "How does it look?"

Lana's face lit up. "It looks great! You look great!"

Standing, Evan stepped in front of the dresser and looked in the mirror. Then, quickly going from the bedroom to where his leather trench coat hung by the door, he slipped the coat on and hurried back to the bedroom.

His eyes sparkled as he looked in the mirror. It was perfect. He was perfect.

"Wow! That looks great!" Lana pulled the quilt around her, slipped from the bed and stood beside him.

Evan turned and took her into his arms; then, he kissed her. "Thank you."

# Chapter 6

**Lana** was amazed at how good Evan's hat looked; though, compared to him, she felt washed up and unattractive. So, avoiding her image in the mirror as she quickly scooted by it, she hopped in the shower then dressed in the clothes he had bought her: mid-length navy blue skirt, matching leggings, boots and a cream-colored turtleneck.

He had even bought her underwear. The thought of him picking out her panties made her blush. However, he was right; everything looked and fit great. He had good taste.

Evan's coat and new hat hung by the door while they both sat at the table gobbling down plates full of chicken and dumplings. Evan just watched her as he placed another dough ball in his mouth, chewed and swallowed.

Suddenly, the sound of Ches's jeep, pulling up in front of the cabin, made the food Evan had just placed in his mouth go cold.

He could sense the ire in Ches's blood and the rise in his body temperature from where he sat. Ches had come for a fight.

Quickly, placing his fork on the table, he looked over at Lana who had sensed it too.

"Lana, go into the bedroom."

"But, Evan...."

Suddenly, Ches burst through the front

door; however, Evan was already on his feet.

Quickly, he scaled the space between them and shoved Ches back out onto the porch.

"Go home, Ches."

Ches caught hold of the railing and shoved Evan back. "No!" he angrily shouted. "I wanna' talk to Lana—see what you've done to her."

"What the hell are you talking about? I didn't do anything to her!"

They stood toe to toe, their faces inches apart. Imaginary darts shot from them both as their eyes flared between red and black and their bodies tensed, preparing for transformation.

Diana suddenly rushed from inside her cabin. Evan's gaze cut in her direction. Somehow, he felt she was responsible for Ches being there.

"What did you say, Diana?" Evan demanded. What did you tell him?"

Her eyes turned hateful. "I just told the truth! And, I didn't even tell Trey about ya'll comin' home the other night all bloody. Ya'll have been gettin' into trouble and it's all because of Lana! Get rid of her, Evan. I want her outta' here!"

"What?" Ches grabbed Evan's shirt.

Evan angrily shoved Ches's hand away. "Get your hands off me! If it's a fight you want, it's a fight you'll get."

"As arachnids?" Ches asked.

"No," Evan replied. "As man-to-man."

"Stop!" Lana cried. Hurrying from inside, she quickly squeezed between them. "I'm okay, Ches. You have to stop."

Tearing his gaze from Evan, he looked at

her; hurt was hiding in the fury that began to alter his normally gentle eyes.

"Lana, what's going on here? I told you this was no good for you." He softly touched her face with his forefinger.

"Get your hands off her!" Evan snapped as he pushed Ches's hand away.

Ches tensed and his fists curled. "I'll touch her if I want to!"

"Evan, stop!" Lana's voice trembled as she grabbed his arm. "Just give me a few minutes to talk to him."

Evan's dark gaze narrowed. "Fine." Turning, he angrily walked inside; the wooden floor cracked beneath his feet as he made his way to the kitchen.

Lana took Ches's hand. "Come on, Ches; take a walk with me. We need to talk."

Ches's gaze shot from her to Evan standing in the kitchen. "Sure," he answered. His body was tense, ridged, and his adrenaline had reached the roof. More than anything, he wanted to take Lana into his arms, carry her to his jeep and drive, drive to the ends of the earth if he had to, just far away from here.

His thoughts also toyed with the idea of transforming, wrapping her in his webbing, then racing through the forest to disappear and never be seen again.

Gently, he squeezed her hand.

They walked in silence toward the forest and stopped approximately fifty feet away from the cabin. The sun was shining brightly; however, the air was crisp.

"Ches...," Lana's voice was soft and low. But, before she could say anther word, he had her in his arms with his face in her hair and his lips pressed lightly to her ear.

"Don't say anything," he softly whispered. "Just listen. For the past few days, I haven't been able to sleep, or eat, or think about anything but you. I've had nightmares about you being here, nightmares of you being attacked by Spence and his goons."

Lana looked at him strangely.

Noticing her look, he pulled away from her and placed his hands on her shoulders. His lips tightened and his gaze narrowed as he stared into her eyes. "Is that what happened? Is that what Diana was talking about. Did you get attacked by Spence again?" His voice had raised an octave.

Lana looked up at him. "Its okay, Ches. We're okay."

"I don't care about Evan," his reply was marked. "He's the one who's getting you mixed up in all this."

He pulled her to him again. "Lana, you have to leave here. Don't you understand?"

"Please, come home with me." Suddenly, he pressed his lips against hers.

Lana closed her eyes as her arachnid beast sparked to life, filled with mixed emotions: confusion and desire, a want for Ches. Or, was it his arachnid male. Lana knew it was wrong. No matter what her inner beast wanted, and no matter how much she cared for and loved Ches, she loved

Evan even more, much more.

She needed to use her powers of persuasion on him—make him realize that she wasn't the best thing for him, that there was someone else out there meant for him. But, who?

Things seemed so unfair. Her mind just couldn't wrap itself around a conclusion that would make everyone happy, especially Ches.

Opening her eyes, she attempted to speak.

"Ches, listen to me."

Her voice was gentle, soft; it was a song upon his ears. He opened his eyes as his heart beat anxiously in his chest and he tasted the sweetness of her breath. He had kissed her before, but not like this. Increasing his grip on her, he lifted her into the air while he continued to gaze into her chestnut-colored eyes.

"Ches..." Lana's lips briefly broke from his as she attempted to speak and gazed into his eyes. His irises were full of color and danced in the sunlight. She never wanted to see him sad and hated herself for having to let him go.

"Ches...you have to let me go."

His lips pressed to hers again, moving with urgency as if he were clinging to her by his mouth.

"No. I can't let you go..." His words were heated upon her tongue and she detested herself for what she was doing.

Suddenly, he paused as if he had been abruptly struck. His head began to spin; and, for a brief moment, the beast within him burned as an ignited fire, burned for her.

"Lana, what are you doing to me?" He

thought he would explode, possibly even tear her to shreds.

Then, as quickly as the feeling appeared, it disappeared, and his body became numb. His eyes were filled with confusion.

"Lana?" His hands grasped at her, as his body slipped to the ground.

"Ches," she whispered gently into his ear. Tears welled at the back of her eyes as she thought of the possibility of never seeing him again; her heart was tearing in two.

Swallowing, she quietly spoke, "Ches..."

**Diana** observed Ches and Lana from the corner of her cabin. She had watched them kiss and could slightly hear Ches's pleas. Her gaze whipped between them and Evan's door as she watched for any sign of Evan. Hurtful anger stiffened her shoulders and banged within her skull; and, unable to control herself any longer, she marched across the yard, up the steps of Evan's cabin and went inside.

Evan was standing in the kitchen. His back was to her and his head hung as he spoke.

"What is it, Diana?"

She shook with rage and her southern drawl spiked with each word. "I want her outta' here, Evan. I mean it! My father owns this here property and I want her out!"

"No, Diana. She's not going anywhere," he replied wearily. "She's staying."

"Damn ya'll, Evan! I'll talk to my father about this and he'll make that little two-timin' freak leave."

"No, Diana, he won't. Grandmother Hobbs gave me this cabin and its mine. She left it to me in her will."

"And, how did ya'll explain that one, Evan? She'd never even known ya'll back then. That was too long ago according to Daddy. Don't ya'll think he'da thought somethin' was up?"

"No," he replied wearily. "It was willed to a grandson of an acquaintance of Grandmother Hobbs; and, that grandson is me. It also stated that I was to retain a job. So, no. Lana is not leaving."

Suddenly, his head snapped up and his near black gaze shot past her to the open door. He listened closely to what he knew was Lana's heart beat. It, along with her temperature, had increased somewhat earlier; however, right now, they were skyrocketing. And, so was Ches's.

"Ches!" In a flash, Evan was out the front door and across the yard where Lana and he were. Ches was on his knees clinging to her.

"Ches!" Evan grabbed him by the arm.

Lana's concentration broke. "Evan, stop!"

Ches dropped to all fours. He was panting. "Oh, my god. What was that?"

Ignoring him, Evan turned to Lana and took her hand. "Come inside with me." He added, "Please. This is too dangerous; and, I don't like the idea of you being alone with him."

He began to lead her across the yard.

"But..." Lana protested, "he wasn't trying to hurt me..."

He cut her off. "Then, what was he doing that made your heart race and your temperature soar?" The look on her face answered the question for him.

"Never mind..." He turned to head back into the cabin when, suddenly, Ches tackled him from behind.

"Let her go!"

Evan stumbled forward and dropped to his hands and knees on the ground. Rage tightened his body in knots as his eyes flashed between red and black; and, his nostrils flared as he spoke.

"Ches..." Each one syllable word was clipped, "...let me go."

Without waiting for a response, Evan spun and landed upright on his feet. His eyes burned as he watched Ches also leap to his feet and settle into a fighting stance.

"So, this is what you wanna' do?" Evan's eyes narrowed and his brow furrowed.

Ches shook his head, still mildly recovering from Lana's eye control. "Lana, you may want to go inside," he stated as he looked at her. His gaze then shot back to Evan as he spoke. "I'd do anything for her. Anything. Even if that means kicking your sorry butt."

"No! Don't do this!" Lana cried; her large eyes were pleading as she turned to Evan, then back to Ches. Maybe she could use her eye control? Make them stop. She knew Evan would never back down, he was too stubborn. Maybe, she could use it again on Ches.

"Ches, please, look at me."

Ches's gaze was locked with Evan's and he knew what she was trying to do.

If the situation were different, he would have loved to again experience what she had just done. He had felt invigorated and drained all at the same time; while the beast within him had been rapidly loosened, then reigned under control.

"No, Lana." He mildly chuckled. "I loved what you did with your eyes; and, I'd love to try it again. However, under different circumstances and when we're alone."

# Chapter 7

**"Hey,** Trey." Several familiar faces smiled and waved as Trey climbed from his vehicle and headed toward the registration building. If Ches didn't register today, they may not have any classes together.

"Ches, you knucklehead," he whispered beneath his breath as he pasted a smile to his own face and waved back.

Suddenly, his cell phone began to ring. It was Diana. Ches and Evan were fighting.

**Evan** had heard enough.

"Ches!" His bare feet skimmed the ground as he spun and executed the perfect roundhouse kick. However, Ches was ready and he hurriedly blocked it.

Evan wasn't surprised. They both had extraordinary strength and speed from being arachnids; and, he knew this wouldn't be an easy fight.

Ches grinned. "Man, you're pretty quick; but, you're gonna' have to be a little quicker than that to beat me, Evan Labonte."

Throwing one punch after another, Ches fired off blow after blow at Evan's face. Suddenly, he clipped Evan with an upper cut to the jaw.

"Ugh!" Evan's head snapped back and he stumbled to regain his footing.

Ches stepped from side to side. He smirked. "Does that hurt?"

Evan's eyes burned black as he swiped the back of his arm across his bleeding lip. Ches's niggling remarks were driving him crazy, making him furious. His fists shook with rage as he again charged toward Ches; and, though Ches was slightly larger than he, he was quicker. He would have to move fast, yet accurately, make every move count.

He wanted this fight to be over with and Ches as far away from him and Lana as possible.

Evan rapidly spun, cracking Ches alongside the head with his foot.

Ches grimaced. "Yeah, that hurt."

"Good," Evan growled, "then I'll do it again."

Two more kicks landed Ches's face and head. "Ugh!" Ches blocked the next blow; however, missed the back flip that sent Evan's two feet ramming into his stomach.

Doubling over, he gasped for a breath while Evan continued to come at him, sending one kick after another in his direction. Suddenly, grabbing Evan by the ankle, Ches twisted it and sent Evan flying face first to the ground.

Evan cursed as blood bubbled along the scratches now covering his face. This was going to end and end quickly.

They were now close to the cabin. Quickly scaling the side to the roof, Evan dove upon Ches, sending them both tumbling backward to the earth with Evan landing on top. Evan threw one punch after another at Ches.

Suddenly, Lana's screaming tore into his concentration on the fight.

"Evan, no!" She was only a few feet away.

"Lana! Get back!" he yelled.

"No, stop!" She stepped closer.

Suddenly, Ches, using the distraction to his advantage, curled up and sent his forehead smashing into Evan's.

"Gah!" An explosion of stars burst within Evan's head and, for a moment, he couldn't see. Scrambling backward, he awkwardly got to his feet.

Ches also scurried to standing and settled into a fighting stance. His nose was bleeding and his eyes were beginning to swell. He swayed unsteadily with his fists held before him and watched as Evan did the same.

"Both of you, stop!" Lana moved even closer.

"Lana..." Evan breathed, "...you have to get back."

"No! I won't let you do this."

Ches ran the back of his sleeve across his bloodied nose. "Ow," he involuntarily yelped. "He's right, Lana. You have to get back."

"No." She stepped between them. "You have to stop fighting."

Suddenly, their heads turned in unison at the sound of Trey's charger coming up the road. Then, Evan and Ches's gaze returned to lock.

Diana quickly scooted from her front steps,

where she had been watching the fight, and hurried to Trey's car. She had called him and told him everything.

"They all been fightin' like two rabid racoons." She pointed her finger in Ches and Evan's direction.

Trey opened his door and climbed out. Observing the situation, he called over to his friend, "Ches—are you okay?"

Ches exhaustedly waved him away. "I'm fine." He wiped the beads of sweat from his forehead.

"You don't look fine, buddy. You're face is black and blue and your nose looks like a tangerine from here. What did I always say about protecting your face?"

Ches's hand was waved in his direction again.

Another car was driving up the road; it was a Subaru. Evan glanced over to see who it was; and, though his head was still buzzing and his vision wasn't one hundred percent, he knew it was Jacob Winslow. Lucinda and the twins were in the car with him.

"Great," Evan grumbled. He held a hand up to Ches. "Give me a minute."

Ches waved a hand at him also.

Jacob climbed from the car. "Lucinda, you and the children stay in the car."

Lucinda's thin brows arched and she meekly smiled as she nodded her head in understanding.

"Awww, but Mamma," Aimery and Aimee whined, "Uncle Evan's fighting and we wanna' watch!" Their father's dark stare shot in their direction.

"Ssh." Lucinda pressed a finger to her lips. "Your father needs to speak to Uncle Evan and then we have to get home. Remember..." She smiled warmly. "...we have ice cream in the back."

"Well, if we don't get to see Uncle Evan today, can we come back?" They chimed in unison.

"Yes, of course," she assured them. "And, maybe you could help him stack some wood?" She winked at the two.

"Blah!" Aimery turned his head and stuck his tongue out. "Ew, work!"

"I'll come and help Uncle Evan stack wood," Aimee volunteered in her soft voice. "I like helping Uncle Evan."

Lucinda brushed a strand of long scarlet hair from Aimee's face. "I know you do, sweetie. And, I'm sure he would love having you around." She smiled again; then, she listened closely to the conversation between her husband and Evan.

Evan rubbed his dirty hands along the sides of his jeans; then, he wiped the sweat and blood away from his face with the corner of his shirt.

Walking to where Jacob stood next to the car, he stuck out his hand.

"Jacob..."

"Evan..." Jacob ignoring his outstretched hand, just nodded his head as a dark scowl shadowed his face.

Evan immediately lowered his hand. He knew Jacob was unhappy about Lucinda and the twins being here around the fighting, and, it might even affect his decision about helping him get Samuel out of Brant. But, what could he do; he certainly hadn't planned on getting into a brawl with Ches today.

Jacob's black eyes cut to Ches, then to Lana where his stare remained. "You have another male here, an arachnid male, around a female?"

Evan glared at him. "Not by choice."

"You endanger us all, Evan Labonte."

Evan's ire had reached its boiling point; he'd had enough for one day.

"Look, Jacob, did you come here to lecture me, or do you have an answer as to whether or not you're going into Brant?"

"Well, by the look of things, you do need a lecturing once in awhile. And, how is it that the number of arachnids is growing, especially around you? This place reeks of black widow blood. And, that female..."

"Lana. Her name is Lana," Evan interrupted.

Jacob's lip curled while his dark stare shot to Evan. "Whatever her name is, her scent is extremely pungent. And, if there are others out there, which I undoubtedly think there are, you're going to have a massive bloodbath on your hands. Any male within five miles of her can smell her."

Evan glanced over at Lucinda who was closely watching her husband. He knew that Jacob was more concerned over Lucinda than about him and Lana. For, he could see through the window of the vehicle that Lucinda's stomach had gotten somewhat larger since the last time he had seen her. Giving Evan a wan smile, she offered a wave of encouragement. Then, she turned her attention to Aimery who was teasing his sister.

Jacob continued. "If we go in, I suggest you leave her behind."

Evan's brow furrowed. "So, you're going in?"

"Yes," Jacob responded as he turned and looked at his family sitting in the car. "We can't allow those at Brant to continue with these experiments. Like you, they endanger us all. They need to be shut down. And, the more the military finds out about us, the more risky it will be for all those arachnids who already exist."

"And, what if there are others?" Evan's brows rose to beneath his disheveled hair.

Jacob just looked at him; his dark eyes were void and unreadable. "We'll deal with that bridge if and when we come to it." Then, he turned on his heels, walked the short distance to the driver's door and opened it.

The chattering twins immediately became silent as their father spoke.

"I'll be here at dawn." Slipping behind the wheel, he started the car, backed around and headed out the long drive.

Evan briefly watched them go as Aimery waved excitedly to him and Aimee blew him a kiss. He waved and returned Aimee's gesture.

Giggling, Aimee then spun around in her seat, and the car disappeared out of sight.

# Chapter 8

**Evan's** stare darkened as his black iris voo-doo shot to Ches who was now sitting on the front steps of the cabin. Lana had gotten him a plastic bag full of ice and was standing before him, doc-toring him like a mother does a small child.

Evan hollered over to Trey who was stand-ing with Diana next to his car.

"Trey, will you please take him home."

Trey shrugged his shoulders theatrically. "If he'll go with me, I'd be more than happy to."

Handing the bag of ice to Lana, Ches stood to his feet. His bloodshot eyes were now encircled by dark yellow-blue rings. "No," he stated. "We'll finish the fight." His breaths were measured and he could barely stand.

"Ches," Lana took his arm; and, before he could turn his head, she caught his gaze.

His eyes were puffed and discolored and his nose continued to bleed. And, though she knew he would heal within a few hours, her heart ached at his pain and discomfort.

Locking her eyes with his, she softly spoke. "Ches, you have to quit fighting. Please."

Evan watched from a distance. And, though, he remained alert to Ches's actions, he didn't want to watch. So, passing the two, he headed into the cabin. He knew what Ches was experiencing while being under Lana's spell. It was a compilation of feelings that nearly drove the male arachnid crazy. Evan's body stiffened at the thought. Ches needed to leave, and, leave soon.

Within a few moments, Lana was quickly ascending the steps to enter the cabin.

Evan stood in the bathroom before the mirror, wiping the dirt and blood from his face while taking care to watch the scratches and the lump on his forehead. He had removed his dirty shirt and his shoulders and muscles were tense, tightened like cords of steel. His jeans were stained and his hair was mussed. He spoke to her reflection.

"Where's Ches?"

Lana softly responded, "He's sitting in his jeep with Trey."

Evan remained quiet for a minute as tension filled the small space between them.

"I'm going in for Samuel in the morning." He turned to look at her. His voice and demeanor were emotionless, nearly cold. "And, while I'm gone, you need to make a decision whether or not you want to stay here with me or be with Ches."

Lana took a step toward him. "You know I wanna' be with you."

Evan put his hand out to stop her from coming any closer. "Then, why do you let him kiss you?"

His stare was dark and a slight shiver ran down Lana's spine as he continued.

"Lana, don't you understand how dangerous this is? If one of us releases his arachnid beast, the other is dead..."

An image of her in human form, trying to stop him and Ches from fighting, entered her mind. Shaking her head, she softly whispered, "I would never let that happen."

Evan tossed the hand towel to the vanity top. His look was incredulous. "And, you think you can stop it? Stop two black widows from fighting over you? Look at me, Lana."

Her gaze fell on his face which appeared as stone, then, ran the length of his body. He was pointing to the red markings lining his sides.

"As long as I have these and can transform into an arachnid, I am nothing more than a beast. And, I can not guarantee that when it comes to another male being around you that I won't turn into that beast and kill someone."

Sadness raced to Lana's eyes. "No, Evan." Her words were choked as she spoke, "You're not a beast. You're Evan Labonte; and, I love you. I love you more than anything."

Stepping forward, she grabbed him around the waist and laid her cheek against him. His chest was hard, yet warm and comforting.

Evan's arms slipped around her and he pulled her close. "It's taken me all these years to find someone—find you. And, I'm sorry that things are so complicated." He took her face into his hands and looked into her dampened eyes. "But, I can't be around you as long as Ches is. It's too dangerous for everyone, especially for you."

His hands slipped to his sides.

"What are you saying?" She reached for his

hand; however, he pulled it away. Her grip went to the vanity to help her remain steady, while she couldn't believe what she was hearing. And, if her heart were a china doll's, it would have shattered to pieces.

Her trembling voice echoed in his name. "Evan?"

His demeanor was set and his manner cool as he walked past her and out of the bathroom. "I have to take care of some things before tomorrow."

Lana stood alone, trying to rationalize his actions. Her legs felt weak; and, the chicken and dumplings she had consumed earlier felt as if they were lodged in the back of her throat.

Trey suddenly appeared at the front door; and, seeing the stricken look on her face, he asked, "Lana? Are you okay?"

Silently, she nodded her head as tears began to flow from her eyes.

His irate stare shot in the direction of Evan's back. "No. You're not okay."

Evan turned, and entering the bedroom, quickly closed the door.

Trey stepped forward and wrapped his arms around her. And, recalling how she transformed when she cried, he quickly asked, "Are you going to transform?"

She shook her head and wiped the tears from her eyes. "No, I can control it now."

He smiled. "Well, that's good." He lightly patted the back of her hair, then released her as he whispered, "Do you wanna' talk about it?"

"No. I just need for you to take Ches home."

"Easier said than done. But, I'll try." His look turned serious as he glanced down at her and his voice was low. "He's really in love with you, Lana."

"I know," she replied as she sniffled. "I'm sorry about that."

He lightly laughed and smiled wide. She had never noticed before how good looking he actually was.

"That's not your fault." He touched her shoulder. "If it weren't for those two knucklehead's fighting over you, I might go for ya' too."

Color shaded Lana's cheeks and she quickly changed the subject.

"They're going into Brant tomorrow. Evan's certain Samuel's there and they're going to try and get him out."

The bedroom door opened and Evan appeared.

Suddenly, Trey felt uncomfortable.

"Evan, ya' want some help tomorrow?" he hurriedly volunteered.

"No. Jacob and I can manage. However, I do need to get a shower." His gaze shot to Lana; then, he quickly looked away. "Oh, and Trey...make sure Ches doesn't come back here again. I went easy on him today. Next time, I may not be able to restrain myself."

"Right," Trey responded, as he placed his index finger to his temple and imitated a salute. Then, glancing at Lana, he turned and headed back outside.

An awkward silence filled the bathroom.

"I wanted to thank you for the clothes," she announced out of the blue.

"You're welcome," Evan replied.

Leaving the room, Lana quietly closed the door behind her. Her body trembled with the thought of Evan not wanting to be with her. It was the same feeling she had when he first left her at Trey's house. She couldn't allow that to happen again; she loved him too much and couldn't stand the idea of being without him. She would have to talk to Ches, get him to go home.

Wiping any evidence that she had been crying from her eyes, she went outside.

Ches was standing next to his jeep along with Trey and Diana. He watched her from behind a mask of black and blue, yellow and green; and, his nose was now bandaged. Diana must have seen to that.

Lana silently noted her gratitude as she walked in their direction.

Diana angrily stared at her, attempting to bore holes into her skin. Then, she snapped, "Are ya'll happy now?"

"Diana," Trey touched her arm. "Don't."

"And, why not?" Diana's incessant glare cut to him. "Look at all the trouble that there little tart's caused."

"Diana!" Ches shouted. "That's enough!" His hand immediately shot to his nose. "Ow."

"You're right, Diana." Lana looked from Ches then to Trey while trying to avoid the imaginary shards flying from Diana's icy stare. "I'm sorry for all the trouble I've caused. I wish I could change it;

but, I can't."

Ches touched her arm. "Lana..."

Lana's gaze locked with his. The situation was heartbreaking; and, seeing him like this made it even worse.

Momentarily, she closed her eyes against the tears that were forming behind her lids; and, when she opened her eyes, she stated with finality, "I need you to go home, Ches." The words seemed to be tearing a hole in her heart as she said them. "I want you to leave."

"Lana, please." He grabbed her arm and his eyes frantically searched hers. "Don't do this."

"Ches...you have..."

Trey touched his arm. "Ches, come on man. Let's go home. You can get cleaned up."

Ches yanked away as his hurtful gaze held to Lana's teary eyes. "Is this what you really want?"

Swallowing back the lump that was still lingering in her throat, Lana looked to the ground and answered. Her one syllable word was barely a whisper. "Yes."

A round moment passed as Ches studied her face and she wiped her eyes with the back of her hand.

"Okay," he said. "But, I'm not giving up. I love you, Lana." He took her chin in his hand. Her spilling tears were too much to bare. "Evan's won this round; however, the next one he won't."

Slowly, his hand slipped from her face. Then, turning he walked around to the driver's side of his jeep and hopped in.

The jeep roared to life as Ches gunned the

motor. His heart was roaring identically within his chest, aching with excruciating pain. Looking back at Lana, he threw the shifter into first and tore out the road.

Trey turned to Diana. He smiled wanly. "I'd better go and make sure he's all right."

Diana only nodded; then her glare shot again to Lana. "Ya'll have ruined everybody's life."

Then, spinning on her heels, she marched up her cabin steps and went inside.

# Chapter 9

**Though** Evan had his back to Lana when she left the bathroom, he had listened to her every breath, every heartbeat and every bat of an eyelash. Why did things have to be so complicated?

He banged his fist on the back of the door. "Damn it!" Then, removing his clothes, he turned the shower on, adjusted the temperature to extra warm and stepped in.

The water ran hot along his skin and caressed his tightened muscles; and, putting his head back, he allowed the water to run over his face and wet his hair. Normally, he hated it; however, today it felt extremely good. Then, finishing up in the shower, he dressed and made his way to the living room.

Lana was sitting quietly on the couch, fidgeting nervously as he entered the room.

Ches's scent was no longer present; he was long gone. Good, Evan thought—one problem solved.

"I have to go see Diana. She and I have never fought like this before." His tone was flat, as if he were speaking to an empty room. Lana's stare was hurtful and he tried to avoid it; however, it wasn't easy.

"Will you be gone long?" she quietly asked.

"I don't know," he stated matter-of-factly. "For as long as it takes, I guess." Then, before she could respond, he opened the door and stepped outside.

Darkness had come and the air was cool and crisp. Evan took a deep breath. He thought that the fight with Ches had been, to an extent, troublesome—possibly even annoying. However, he knew that dealing with Diana would be even worse.

Shoving his hands in his pockets, he walked down the steps and over into her yard. A small light was lit in her kitchen and he could hear her meandering around inside.

Inhaling deep, he scaled her steps two-at-a-time and knocked on the door. A moment passed and she opened it and stepped outside. Her demeanor was reserved, veiled by her distant gaze and a forced smile.

"May I come in?" he asked.

"I guess," she replied as she turned. Evan followed her inside.

Diana's cabin was an exact replica in layout of Evan's; however, hers had a window in the kitchen and one in the living room. Plus, she had more furniture and accessories. He had to admit it was decorated beautifully with several vases of fresh flowers sitting in various locations—the kitchen table, a pedestal, and the counter separating the kitchen from the living room. One would have never guessed it could have been so lovely from the outside.

Diana sat down on an overstuffed navy loveseat while she gestured for Evan to sit in the matching recliner opposite her. She had tied her hair up, while several loose strands cascaded along her slender cheeks to the length of her chin, and her eyes shone like blue diamonds. Evan had to admit; she was beautiful.

Diana's gaze shot to him as she crossed her perfect legs and her short skirt slid slightly up her thighs. Then, she turned her body in his direction.

Evan slipped into the chair and took a deep breath.

"Is there somethin' ya'll wanna' say, Evan?"

His hands wrung as he began and his eyes dropped to watch them. "Well, I just wanted to try and clear the air."

Glancing out of the corner of his eye, he attempted to view the look upon her face. It hadn't changed since he had come in; and, the silence she continued to embrace was nerve-racking.

Looking directly at her, he continued. "I know we've been friends for a long time; but, that's what it's been...good friends."

Thunderclouds of rage drifted across her face, attempting to quickly hide the hurt that had suddenly shadowed her features. "I always thought it was more than that." Her accent twisted as she spoke. "I've loved you all these years, Evan. All these years!"

Her gaze cut to the wall as she stood and tears surged to her eyes. They streamed her cheeks as she spoke each word. "I tried to love ya'll as a sister, but it doesn't work!"

Evan stood to his feet and crossed the few

steps between them. He needed to console her, show her how bad he felt about the situation.

Diana pushed him away and began to pace. Then, halting in her tracks, she spun to face him. Her tone suddenly sweetened as she spoke. It was as if she were a Doctor Jekyll, Mr. Hyde. "Evan, please. Please don't do this."

Quickly, she spanned the small space between them; and, lunging at him, she knocked him backward onto the couch.

"Diana..."

Her mouth covered his and her pleading words rushed upon his lips. "I'll do anythin' ya'll want. Anythin'." She pressed her body tightly to his as her aching heart raced in her chest and she became desperate.

"No, Diana. I'm not doing this." Grabbing her shoulders Evan looked into her eyes which were brimming with pain. "This isn't gonna' work."

Diana paused and pushed herself up with her hands. She studied his gaze, trying to find an inkling of love for her in his beautiful kaleidoscopic eyes. However, his stare told her something else— told her something she did not want to hear.

Diana then spoke; her words were hushed, almost inaudible. "When things are over between ya'll and Lana, I'll be waitin', Evan Labonte." Pausing for a moment, she then continued. "Because, I know that deep down inside ya'll love me. Ya'll just don't know it yet."

Quietly, she lifted herself off him and smoothed her disheveled hair and clothes.

"Ya'll are the only person who can make me

forgit myself—forgit that I'm a Hobbs. And, that's sayin' a lot. That's why I can't let ya'll go."

She walked toward the door and opened it. "Now, I think ya'll should leave."

Evan rose from the couch, straightened his clothing and made his way to the door. He turned his head to apologize, attempt to say something that would fix the situation; however, he couldn't. Instead, he gently touched her shoulder, walked past her and out into the night. The door quickly closed behind him.

Glancing back, he shook his head.

Yes, Diana was right about one thing—he did love her. However, it wasn't as a lover or a girl-friend, it was as a good friend—his best friend. And, though she was gorgeous, a creature of beauty, the thought of sleeping with her had never entered his mind. He assumed that it was because she resembled Grandmother Hobbs when Grand-mother had been much younger. That would've been extremely unnerving.

He also considered the severe tongue lash-ing he would have been subjected to if Diana had known he'd slept with other females, both young-er and older than he. The green-eyed monster she possessed would have surely stomped him or had him for dinner.

Exhaling, he briefly stared into the darkness. He wondered how his life might be different in the next five, or ten, or possibly even twenty years. Di-ana would be nearing forty in twenty years; surely she wouldn't continue to pursue him then. She most likely would have a husband and children by that time.

Then, he thought of Lana and how she probably would age as he had, slowly, one year to every ten years of human life. They could grow old together—experience things that others had never known existed, do all those things he could have never shared with anyone else. All of a sudden, he needed to see her.

His pace quickened as he headed home.

**Lana** sat quietly in the living room, listening for Evan's returning footfalls. And, though it had only been a few minutes since he left, it felt like an eternity.

Suddenly, her heart skipped a beat as she heard him coming up the steps. He was alone; however, the smell of Diana's perfume lingered upon him like smoke from a smelly cigar. She wrinkled her nose.

Normally, she loved the scent of a good perfume; but, since her sense of smell had been heightened drastically, she no longer enjoyed it—especially if it was Diana's.

Evan walked in the door. And, though the lighting from the faint lamp shone upon his vibrant eyes and dark wavy hair, making him appear gorgeous, Lana couldn't help but stare at the red lipstick smeared on his face.

He and Diana had been kissing.

Her heart sank within her chest, dropped to her stomach hard, like a bowling ball; and, all the hope she had inside her quickly disappeared. She wanted to cry—do something other than just sit there. The words she then spoke were more to her benefit than truthfully to inquire as to Diana's welfare. It really was to help her breathe.

Inhaling deep, she quietly asked, "Is Diana still mad?"

"No. I guess not." He didn't elaborate, just continued to stand at the door and watch her.

The tension between them was killing her. Lana got up. Her voice was low. "I'm going to bed." She crossed the room to where he was and went to pass him; however, he grabbed her arm and stopped her from entering the bedroom.

"Lana..."

The tears she worked so hard to restrain burst to her eyes.

"Evan, I can't do this," she mumbled. "I know what you and Diana were doing. You have lipstick on your face and her perfume is all over you."

Releasing her arm, he quickly slipped into the bathroom, turned on the light and looked in the mirror.

"Ugh!" He hurriedly grabbed the hand towel and irritably scrubbed at his mouth. "She instigated this; she attacked me." Checking his face for any other marks, he then turned and looked at her.

Her voice shook as she lowly spoke and the tears rolled down her cheeks. "I think you're lying, Evan. You two are always kissing." She turned to go into the bedroom; however, he quickly reached for her and spun her to him.

"Lana, stop." He pulled her tightly to his chest and looked into her tear-filled eyes. "I would never lie to you. I love you."

He placed his lips to hers and kissed her passionately. The taste of her sweet breath and tears intermingled upon his pallet and he wanted more.

She kissed him back, while the urgency to be with him was torturous. Her mind suggested that it was her black widow that was causing her temperature to rise and her head to spin. However, as his lips pressed against hers with want and desire, she knew that it was more than just her inner beast; it was love.

Suddenly, she sneezed, then sneezed again and again.

"Is it the perfume," he asked as he regretfully released her and sniffed at his clothes. She nodded her head and sneezed once more, then wiped her eyes with the back of her hand.

Scowling, he stated, "I'll get in the shower again." Then, he looked down at her and wiped a finger along her wet lash. "I was wrong. I can't stand to be away from you for a minute. I'll be out in just a second." Releasing her, he disappeared into the bathroom.

Through the thick of the wood, Lana could hear him undress. She also heard him grumbling beneath his breath, cursing Diana for being such a menace.

The water spurted from the showerhead and he quickly stepped in. After a moment, Lana then opened the bathroom door and stepped inside.

"Lana?" Evan's brows met as he frowned.

"It won't take me long. I'll be right out." He could faintly hear her above the roar of the water shooting from the spigot. Maybe she really needed to use the bathroom, he thought. Palming shampoo into his hair, he continued to wash.

Suddenly the shower curtain cracked open; and, out of the blue, she was undressed and stepping in.

"What are you doing," he quietly asked as he forced his gaze to remain focused on her face.

For a moment, she was quiet, all of a sudden embarrassed by her actions. Her voice was low as she spoke, just like a child who had just gotten caught with its hand in the cookie jar. "I want to be with you..." Her eyes swam with emotion as the water ran over her face and hair and she fidgeted nervously. "Is that okay?"

# Chapter 10

**Lana** watched Evan as he tilted his head back and smiled. Tiny shampoo bubbles ran from his wavy strands of hair to his broad shoulders and chest.

She couldn't help but be mesmerized by them, how easily they flowed along his body without reserve or care. However, she dared not to avert her stare from his face, neck and chest—keep her gaze above his ribcage. Gathering her courage, she suddenly stepped forward and wrapped her arms around him.

Evan's eyes sparked and he smiled as he looked down at her face and watched as the water ran over them both. His arms slipped around her and fell at the small of her back. Gently, he pulled her closer. Her body slightly tensed.

"Are you sure about this?" he asked.

Her eyes were wide and she blinked her long lashes at the water droplets that rested upon them. Silently, she nodded her head.

Turning the water off, Evan reached through the curtain, grabbed a towel and gently wrapped it around her. Then, lifting her slender body into his arms, he carried her into the bedroom.

The room was dark except for the glow of a small lantern that was lit upon the dresser.

For some odd reason, Lana felt more at ease in this room. It had become a haven for them both, a place away from the madness of the outside world. A place they could be to themselves and be themselves.

Droplets of water ran from each of their bodies and pattered softly upon the wooden floor adding to the thunderous drums banging in Lana's chest. She thought her heart would burst right through her body.

Laying her gently on the bed, Evan continued to look into her eyes, read her every thought, and her every feeling. Carefully, he removed her towel and dropped it to the floor. He didn't have to look beyond her face; he knew everything was beautiful, beautiful beyond compare.

Quietly, he slid onto the bed beside her. Immediately, she tensed.

"We don't have to do this, you know." His kind words were a whisper. "We can wait." He brushed a strand of damp dark hair away from her face.

Lana looked up at him. His eyes portrayed kindness, sincerity; and, though her body trembled inside, she wanted to be with him more than anything.

"No," she softly spoke, "I wanna be with you—be a part of you."

He quietly laughed. "I could just give you some of my blood."

She blinked. "That's not the same. I want to be with you as your female—be with you forever."

"Forever?" His brows arched. "You know

that's a long time."

She shifted her damp body, careful not to get too close to him.

"Yes, I know," she stated.

"Then, I have something I wanna give you." Reaching for the quilt, he covered them both. Then, pulling a drawer open on his nightstand, he dug beneath his socks; and, finding what he was looking for, he closed the drawer.

In his hand was a small brown leather box which was the size of a man's wallet. The box was old and worn and the leather had been engraved with his name, Evan Labonte. Quickly, he removed the lid and laid it on the nightstand.

"Grandmother had this box made for me." He smiled at the thought. "She had given it to me one Christmas filled with a small bag of chocolates she had made."

Carefully, he reached into it with two fingers and removed the item contained in the box. Then, he held the item before her.

It was a silver ring with a small layer of diamonds cresting the top; and, though it was slightly worn, it shimmered brightly in the dim lighting. Evan looked at her somewhat apologetically.

"It was my mother's wedding ring. Somehow it got caught in my webbing and was stuck to me when I ran away." He spoke more to himself than to her. "It's not a wonder. It always was too big for her."

His gaze turned to her as he rolled on his side to face her. "I would like for you to have it."

Lana stared at the tiny diamonds that sparkled upon it and felt his mother's love that seemed to warm between her fingertips. "I can't take this," she whispered. "It's the only thing you have left from her."

"Please," he smiled lovingly. "This is my promise to you that we will remain together forever." He took her left hand and slid the ring over her ring finger. However, her hands were petite and the ring was entirely too big. Frowning, he then placed it over her index finger. It was a perfect fit.

"I'll have it resized for you." His smile was small yet warm. "And, if you would decide to marry me one day, I'll make sure you have your own ring, something that isn't used."

Lana swallowed back the huge lump in her throat. "Marriage?" she managed to squeak. "Are you asking me to marry you?"

Worry slightly shadowed his face as he studied her every look. "I know you may not be ready right now; but, yes. When you are ready, I would like very much for you to be my wife."

Lana's head spun as she thought about that for a moment. He was asking her to marry him, yet she hadn't even graduated yet—if she would graduate. Her mind galloped in a thousand directions. She needed to breathe.

Evan watched her facial expressions. "Is that a no?"

Her eyes blinked as she found her voice. "I've never even thought about getting married; I've never even dated." She remained quiet for a moment; then, glancing up at him she answered. "But, yes; I would love to be your wife. But, not later...," she smiled warmly, "...right now. I want to be your wife tonight."

Evan propped himself up on an elbow and ran his forefinger along her cheek.

"Right now?" he softly laughed, then eyed her suspiciously. "Is that so you can get a new ring?"

"No." Her face turned serious. "I would never want another ring." She held up her hand before her and watched the tiny diamonds as they danced in the light. "This ring is more special than any you could buy me at the store. I would like to keep this one."

Evan watched her, enjoying the brightness in her eyes and frowns and smiles that lit up her face. Every second of this moment would be etched upon his heart for eternity. For, while he had been with other females through the past century, he was certain he would be spending the rest of his life alone.

Lana turned on her side to face him and looked into his eyes. "I want to be your wife now... because I love you."

"So, are you talking about getting married in a church? It's a little late this evening for that," he noted with a crooked smile.

Her cheeks colored, then she quickly responded. "Well, probably sometime—after we find Samuel," she added lowly. Sadness shadowed her gaze as her eyes left Evan and scanned the dimly lit room.

"Do you think you'll find him tomorrow?"

"Of course I will." He took her hand in his and

stroked the ring upon her finger with his thumb. "I promise."

Lana lightly smiled as her eyes returned to him. Then, she moved her body closer to his.

"Mr. Labonte," her words were a whisper, "I want you to make me your wife tonight."

Evan placed his lips to hers and kissed her. It was soft and tender as he thought about how much he loved her.

"Mrs. Labonte," his voice was hushed, "I swear on all that is within me to love you forever." And, though his inner beast was now rampaging within him, fighting to burst through his skin and ravage the black widow female that Lana harbored inside, he would restrain its animalistic urges and be extra careful not to hurt her.

Gently, he touched her face and looked into her large eyes. They were wide with anxiety, yet radiated with love.

Evan slid his body against hers and touched her dampened skin. The curves that made up her petite form were soft, yet firm; and her scent was amazing, like a bouquet to his senses. She was beautiful—perfect. And, he loved her more than anything.

Placing his lips to her ear and smelling the freshness of her hair, he inhaled deep. "Let me know if I hurt you," he whispered in his faultless voice.

Lana could only nod her head at his words.


**Evan** slowly opened his eyes and glanced around the room. Outside, nocturnal life was chattering exuberantly; daylight hadn't arrived yet. The alarm clock on his nightstand read 4:22 a.m. He had a couple of hours before dawn and Jacob's arrival.

Turning his head, he looked over at Lana curled up tightly against him. He couldn't help but grin.

Quietly, he slid his feet to the floor and grabbed the towel he had wrapped her in the night before; then, he cinched it at his waist. The towel was still slightly damp, but he didn't mind, he felt great; and, nothing bothered him now except the knowledge that he would have to leave her in a few hours.

Heading into the bathroom, he closed the door behind him and switched on the light. Then, running a hand through his mussed hair, he glanced in the mirror. He blinked at what he saw. Besides, his disheveled appearance, blood blotched his body and had dried in crusty patches. It had come from the several bite marks on his neck which were now close to being completely healed.

He knew Lana had bitten him, because it had hurt—hurt like hell. However, he didn't complain. Most likely, she had fought with her inner beast during their love making, aimed to control the black widow while trying to experience and enjoy every moment with him.

Evan touched the small puncture marks on his neck, just thankful she hadn't injected him with any of her poison. She could have easily killed him.

Removing his clothes from where he had

laid them across the commode when getting his shower, he then used the restroom and flushed. The sound of the water rushing through the plumbing seemed much louder than usual. He hoped it wouldn't awaken her; they had been up most of the night.

Turning on the shower, he hopped in. He needed desperately to freshen up, wake up, for the difficult task he was about to undergo. Lana's scent had seeped within his skin and was filling his nostrils with her sweet aroma. He hated to wash it off.

Finishing his shower, he stepped from the tub, dried himself off and dressed. A light knock sounded upon the bathroom door.

"Evan, are you in there?" Lana's tired, soft voice came from the other side.

"Yeah." He quickly opened the door to see her wrapped in his quilt which was now their quilt. He could get used to that.

Yawning, she rubbed her eyes with the back of her hand and pushed the strands of unruly hair away from her face. "Are you coming back to bed?"

"No, I can't; Jacob will be here soon. Then, we'll be heading out."

"But, I don't want you to go." Her lower lip was puffed out.

Evan's brows met. "I think you do."

"I know," she stated. "But, I'm afraid something will happen to you and you won't come back."

"I have a wife to come home to now. I will

definitely be back."

Color fled to Lana's cheeks as she glanced at the ring upon her finger and said, "Thank you."

He looked at her strangely. "Thank you for what?"

"Thank you for rescuing me that day I was attacked in town; and, most of all, thank you for choosing me to be your wife."

Wrapping his arms around her, he drew her close and spoke into the crown of her head. "You don't have to thank me. I should be the one thanking you."

Lana nestled her face in his neck. His collar shifted and the several bite marks he had were exposed. She immediately pulled away.

"Oh, my gosh! Look at your neck!" She touched the wounds lightly with her fingers as her wide eyes shot to his face. "Did I do that?" Without waiting for a response, she whispered, "I'm so sorry. I didn't mean to."

Evan pulled her back toward him while running his fingers through her hair. "Don't be. They're almost healed."

"Do they hurt?"

"Not any more."

"Geez. I'm really sorry. I guess you won't wanna..." Blushing, she paused for the right words.

Evan softly laughed. Then, placing a kiss to both of her eyelids, he stated, "I don't care how often you bite me, I could never say 'no' to being with you."

"So, I make you happy?" she anxiously asked.

Evan grinned and his eyes sparkled. "More

than you'll ever know, Mrs. Labonte."

His hands slipped within the quilt and he lightly touched her skin. It thrummed beneath his fingertips sending tiny electrical currents buzzing to his every extremity. The energy within him soared and suddenly, he needed her, wanted her more than anything.

Scooping her up into his arms, he carried her into the bedroom; and, heeling the door closed behind him, he headed for their bed.

Jacob Winslow would just have to wait.

# Chapter 11

**Evan** had lightly dozed; and, when he awoke, it was to the crashing sound of thunder and lightning. A vicious storm was brewing outside.

"Great," he mumbled as he sat up and reached for his pants on the floor. Lana's hand slid across the sheet to find his.

"It's storming," she softly mumbled as she breathed in and lifted her head. Thunder cracked overhead; it seemed to vibrate the entire cabin. Squealing, she quickly ducked beneath the blanket.

"What's the matter?" he asked as he placed a hand on her shoulder.

Peeking her head out, she slightly whined. Evan thought it was cute.

"I don't like storms." She shrugged her bare shoulders while displaying a jutting lower lip. "They scare me."

He gently embraced her. "It'll be okay. The storm's outside and you're inside."

"But, I'll be here alone, if you leave."

He kissed the top of her forehead. "I'll be back as soon as I can. Besides, spiders don't fare too well in bad weather; their webbing disintegrates quicker and their senses are muddled by the dampness on their body hair. So, Jacob will make this quick."

"Can't you wait until tomorrow?"

"No. When he sets his mind to something, it can't be changed—come hell, or even, high water. In fact, I think his car is outside—at least it sounds like his."

Slipping his pants on, he shuffled to his dresser and quickly grabbed a shirt. Then, he walked out of the bedroom and to the front door.

Evan looked outside. Rain was coming down in buckets, as if the sky had been opened and the heavens released. Thunder pounded overhead and lightning leapt as giant fingers across the sky. The exceptional good mood he was in suddenly disappeared.

It was difficult to see through the rain; and, his sense of awareness and smell was greatly hindered. Narrowing his vision, he attempted to look for Jacob's black Jag, the car Jacob drove when he was out without the twins.

"Hm." He shrugged his shoulders and leaned his head out the door a little farther.

Suddenly, pain raced throughout the entire right side of his face. "What the..." His hand shot up to his cheek. A small dart protruded from his skin. Yanking it out, he briefly stared at it, then tossed it to the ground.

His mind began to whirl, whirl like the winds in a dust storm; and, his eyes were unable to focus. "What's happen..." the mumbled words were abruptly cut short as he toppled forward and his face cracked against the front porch steps. Rain was pouring down, running in his nose and open eyes. He couldn't move.

Several sets of black military boots rapidly ascended the steps. The pounding of their heels echoed within his ears, as they raced toward the inside of the cabin.

"Lana..."

He could hear her scream.

"Leave her alone..." he mumbled through numb, wet lips. "Leave her..."

Suddenly, he was yanked upward and being half dragged and half carried to a dark van and truck sitting beside the cabin in the driveway. Barely able to glance over his shoulder, he caught a glimpse of Lana being dragged outside also.

"Evan!" she cried.

A soldier had her by each arm while she tried desperately to cling to the quilt. Lightning shot in every direction and she screeched at its violent coming.

"No!" Evan struggled against the numbness and the two soldiers holding him. "Get off her!" Another dart pinched at the back of his neck and his eyes shot to the back of his head. Everything went blank.

"Evan!"

"Get her in the truck!" the officer in charge shouted.

"No! Leave us alone!" Lana cried. Webbing was beginning to pour from her tattoo and her eyes flashed from black to red. Tears added to the wetness streaming her cheeks. "I said, 'Leave us alone!'"

Suddenly, her arachnid legs tore through the quilt and her body began to rapidly transform. There was no time for her thought process to re-act, or for her to cry out in pain. Her body was changing and changing fast.

Corporal Anderson, who was acting on or-ders from Brant, shouted above the drumming of rain, "Somebody grab the tranquilizer gun! And, somebody get the net. We're gonna' take this abomination in!"

Lana was now in her arachnid form; and, screeching in rage. She charged toward the cor-poral and the truck.

"Shoot her!" Corporal Anderson growled. "Somebody shoot her ass!"

Lana was quick and deadly as her fangs rap-idly emerged and webbing shot in every direction. Sailing through the air, she landed atop the corpo-ral, sending them both skidding through the mud. Within seconds, she had him wrapped within her cocoon and her fangs were sunk deep within his skin, poison was being injected into his system.

Thoop! Thoop! Two shots discharged from nearby where a sharp-shooter was bent to one knee brandishing a large tranquilizer gun.

Lana's gaze immediately cut in that direc-tion and for a brief moment, she just stared—her eight eyes fixated on the man. Then, dropping the cocoon, she suddenly splashed face first into the mud.

Being awoken by the storm, Diana, still in her nightclothes, had lazily made her way to her front window and looked out.

Daylight was just breaking and she wanted to get up and get started early. The situation with Evan was driving her crazy and she needed to get away for a while, possibly head into Bridgeton where she would grab a latte' and do some shopping. Yes, that's what she would do—shop until she dropped. However, the yucky weather outside made her tired, just wanting to sleep.

Rubbing her eyes, she did a double-take at the sight she saw just outside her cabin window.

Suddenly, her front door burst open and three armed soldiers pushed their way inside.

"What the...?" There was no time for explanations as they grabbed her by both arms.

Diana became enraged. "Ya'll better get your paws off me! Don't ya'll know who I am?"

"Yes, ma'am we do. You're Diana Marie Hobbs, daughter of Mr. Carl Hobbs and great granddaughter to Marianne Hobbs."

Diana's eyes blazed. "Then, ya'll know you'd better let me go right now!"

"Sorry, ma'am but you're going to have to come with us."

"Well then, can ya'll at least let me get changed?" she growled.

"Sorry, ma'am, we can't allow that? However, we will allow you to get a jacket."

Diana yanked her arms free. "Thanks a lot."

Grabbing her raincoat from the nearby coat rack, she slipped it on and pulled her hood up. Then, reaching for her cell phone, which was nearby, she quickly slid it into her pocket and marched outside.

Her gaze cut to Lana's large arachnid form which was now netted and being dragged through the mud by a number of soldiers who were getting her into the truck. The backs of each of their jackets read: B-R-A-N-T in large white letters.

Diana's pink, fuzzy slippers, being sucked at by the mud, nearly ripped from her feet. It blackened her mood. Somebody's gonna' pay for this... the thought festered like acid in the forefront of her mind...and pay big.

"Where's Evan?" she snapped as they led her toward a black van. There was no response, only the pounding of the down pouring rain.

**Jacob** crouched down within the trees in the not too far off distance, observing through a black stare the scene at the cabins. He continued to remain hidden until the vehicles, holding Lana, Evan and Diana hurriedly raced along the muddy road and out of sight.

His gaze darted to where Lucinda sat waiting in the car. She had insisted on coming, which meant the twins had to be left alone at home. It was something he and Lucinda disliked doing, especially since the twins appeared to be no more than small children. However, since Aimery and Aimee were arachnids and nearly a decade old, they agreed it would be okay. The two were very resourceful if need be.

Several moments passed as Jacob, somewhat obscured from the rain, stood and looked around while considering his options. The storm was still going strong. It was now bending trees and sending branches crashing to the ground. Spinning on his heels, he secured his hood against the raging wind and headed toward the car.

Lucinda would be frantic at Evan's capture; for, she shared a special bond with Evan, a bond through his blood. Jacob never liked it; in fact, he despised it. And, had he known the effects the transfusion would have had on her, he would never have injected her with it. He had only done it to save her life.

Well, that was all in the past; and, getting three people out of Brant was priority now. It would require more work, more strategizing; and, he certainly wouldn't be able to do it alone.

"This is the last time, Evan Labonte," Jacob grumbled. "If you get caught again, you're on your own."

Lucinda was sitting in the car anxiously watching the pouring of rain through the flapping windshield wipers, as Jacob quickly approached. A look of disproval shadowed his already solemn features when he opened the car door and slipped inside.

"What's happened?" she asked as she turned in her seat and handed him a small hand towel to dry himself.

"Evan's gone and gotten himself caught again," he stated as he wiped his face and brushed over his hair.

Lucinda gripped at the leather steering wheel while her stomach began to knot. Her mind raced at the repercussions. Then, she turned to her husband and asked. "What are you going to do?"

Jacob's dark eyes were fixed on the rain. She knew better than to interrupt him while he was thinking. However, anxiety was raging war behind her calm façade.

Then, he finally spoke. "Well, I can't go it alone."

"I could help," Lucinda quickly interjected.

Jacob's dark stare cut to her. "No, absolutely not." His gaze then shot to her small rounded belly. She was only one week pregnant though she looked to be several months.

"Then, who else?" she asked.

"Well, when we were here the other day, and Evan was in the middle of his little sparring match, it was against another arachnid, a newly born arachnid. I detest the idea of involving anyone else; however, he may be of some help."

"How will you contact him? You don't even know who he is."

"You're right. However, there were two vehicles sitting in front of Evan's cabin that day; and, if we're lucky, maybe one of them is the guy's. One of their license plates read: H-R-D-A-S-S. Maybe I can ask around town to see if anyone knows whose car that might be."

Lucinda reached over and touched her husband's hand. Fear shadowed her lovely emerald eyes. "Jacob, I'm frightened for Evan and Lana. Promise me you'll get them back."

Jacob gripped her hand tightly as his onyx-colored eyes stared into hers.

"I'll figure something out."

Lucinda lightly nodded her head and quietly stated, "You always do."

# Chapter 12

**Evan** was shackled by iron restraints to the inside of the van. His head was slumped to his chest and he didn't move.

Diana sat across from him, her arms and legs were also bound. Her mud-covered, wet slippers lay on the floor before her while her dirty bare feet rubbed against one another in the attempt to stay warm. Mud was even caked between her toes. It was disgusting. However, she didn't try to wrench it out; it was the only thing keeping her feet from turning to popsicles.

A soundproof, Plexiglas window separated the front seat of the van from the back where she and Evan were. The reason she knew it was soundproof was because she had yelled her fool head off when they first put her in the van, and the two soldiers sitting up front, hadn't even noticed. They were heavily armed with various weapons and ammunition and didn't flinch at the vulgar things she called them. They just continued to scan the road ahead, as if waiting for someone or something to attack.

"Evan! Wake up!" Diana impatiently pounded her barefoot upon the floor of the van. "Wake up!" He didn't stir.

Laying her head back, she groaned. "This is

ya'lls fault, Lana. Ya'll brought this here trouble on all our heads." Her gaze cut to the two men then to her pocket where her cell phone was. With her hands tied behind her back she wouldn't be able to reach it.

"If I can just get my pocket slid around to my hands." She encouraged herself as she pressed her arms tightly against her sides and slid her jacket pocket toward her back. It was more difficult than what she thought.

After several minutes and several tries, she was able to reach her pocket. Slipping her hand in, she quickly grabbed her cell phone and held it securely. Her fingers hovered lightly over the keys; she would have to text. It would be a little awkward; however, after sending nearly a thousand text messages per day, she had become very proficient and would, more than likely, be able to text something understandable. Shoot, who was she kidding, she could text in her sleep.

But, who would she contact—her father or mother? No—absolutely not. If they found out about Evan and what he was, they'd see to it that she'd never see the cabin or him again. And, what if he was detained by the military, or whoever or whatever they were. Their jackets said, "BRANT". Who the hell was Brant anyway? And, would she actually be able to see Evan again? And, why did they want her?

Well, Evan and Lana were easy enough to figure out—they weren't normal. In fact, they were probably worth millions to science, or to the government. The research they could do would be never-ending. It's a wonder they hadn't been taken earlier.

The idea of getting a million dollars for Lana spun through her mind. Man, she thought, why didn't I think of that. Not only could I have gotten rid of Lana, but I could have also added amply to my already bursting savings account. More shopping.

For several minutes, Diana allowed her mind to relish in the thought. Then, she reined in her galloping ideas and forced herself to concentrate on the situation at hand.

The van was traveling at high speed in the direction of Bear Mountain. It hit a pothole and sent her bouncing half-way off the bench she was tied to. She landed crookedly on her rear.

"Geesh!" Her icy stare shot in the direction of the driver. Then, she glanced over at Evan who still lay unconscious. They had injected him with something potent, something that made him completely unresponsive. Suddenly, he looked vulnerable and small, defenseless to anything.

Diana rolled her eyes. "Damnit! Why do I have to love ya'll so much, Evan?" Her words echoed along the walls of the van and resounded within her own ears. Suddenly, she realized the last thing she was going to do was let someone hurt him.

Gripping her cell phone, she hurriedly began to text Trey's cell number. He would know what to do.

**Ches's** jeep angrily gripped at the muddy

road as Ches held his foot to the gas pedal and drove north. He and Trey were headed toward the cabin they had in the mountains. It was a place to go to reflect on life, also hunt, fish and kayak. They had gone there for several weeks after Tricia had passed away. It had slightly helped.

The rain was beginning to slow, just become a sprinkle. However, it had drenched the entire mountainside and the valley below. The river's were running wild, carrying large broken limbs that had been beaten down by the storm. Tiny streams raced across the roads and land, each taking their own unruly course.

"Ches, don't you think you should slow down a little," Trey yelled above the CD player which was blaring something from Nickelback. They were rounding one sharp corner after another at high speed and mud was coating the sides of the jeep and windows. They could barely see ten feet in front of them.

"I mean, I'm the first to like anything that goes fast; but..." Trey glanced over at the speed-ometer, "you're doing almost 80 mph around this mountain. Frankly, I have'ta tell ya': You're scarin' the shit outta' me."

Ches's gaze continued to follow the road; then, he tapped the cloth top to the jeep. "The rain's slowing down."

Trey's gaze narrowed. "I'm not talking about the rain; I'm talking about your driving."

Suddenly, Ches slammed on the brakes.

"What the..." Trey irritably glanced his way. "What's the matter..."

Ches turned down the radio. "Your cell phone's ringing. You'd better answer it."

Trey's head cocked to the side. "You heard that above the music?"

"Yeah," Ches replied sourly.

Trey silently watched him; then, he spoke. "Look, I know you're upset about Lana and I thought this little trip would help you with that. However, wrecking your vehicle and killing me isn't going to solve anything. Remember, I'll die; you won't."

Ches slowly looked at him. "You need to see who called."

Trey scowled. "Now, you're avoiding the subject."

"There is no subject," Ches replied. "Lana's with the dark troll. End of story. And, I'm certainly not going to let anything happen to you." Ches's cobalt stare was set. "Trust me."

"Well, easier said than done," Trey retorted as his irate stare immediately shot in Ches's direction.

"I saw that," Ches remarked.

"Yeah, I know you did."

Ches tromped on the gas and the big knobby tires gripped at the muddy road. They were doing 80mph again.

Trey reached into his jeans pocket and removed his cell phone. Pressing the message button on the keypad, he quickly read through the text Diana had sent him. It read: Trey help...we r in a van heding towrd Bear Mtn...hury!

Anxiety plagued his face and he fought desperately to hide it.

"So, who was it?" Ches asked.

"Oh, just Diana." Trey was never able to lie to Ches. It was impossible, like hiding an elephant in a clothes hamper. He decided to drop the subject.

"What did she want?"

Trey rolled his eyes. He remained silent, unsure as to what he should say that wouldn't cause Ches to do something stupid, like drive down the mountain at 100mph.

Ches slammed on the brakes and asked again, "What did she want?"

Trey's body recoiled in the belted harness he was in. His features twisted in knots. "If you don't stop that, I'm not telling you anything!"

Ches's stare tightened as he leaned toward his friend. "Ya' know, Trey, I am getting kinda' hungry."

Trey's eyes bulged as he pressed himself against the passenger door. "You wouldn't."

An impish grin crossed Ches's face and his eyes sparked as he leaned closer.

"Try me."

"All right, all right!" Trey nearly shouted. "Ya' couldn't just let it go, could ya'!" He took a deep breath. "Diana's in trouble—they're in trouble. And, they're in a van headed toward Bear Mountain."

The silence became deafening. And, after a moment, Ches opened his door and climbed out. They were sitting on a long stretch of straight-away that ran alongside the mountain. Briefly, he looked over the edge.

"Whadrya gonna do?" Trey asked.

"We're gonna go and help," Ches immediately replied as he turned back to the jeep, speedily reached behind his seat, and busied himself gathering rope and his bowie knife.

"Now, hurry up and get out here."

"Well, whaddaya want me to do?" Trey asked as he climbed out the passenger's side and hurried around the jeep. The rain had slowed to a misting and the dark clouds overhead were beginning to disperse.

"Just hold the rope," Ches quickly stated as he handed Trey the bundled line. Then, he shoved his knife into the sheath and tossed Trey the belt. "And, secure this around your waist."

Shouldering the rope, Trey asked, "Bear Mountain's on the other side of the river; do you think we can catch them?" He hooked the belt around his waist. His attention was suddenly caught as Ches commenced to tear through his clothes and begin to transform.

"So, you're going as an arachnid? And, what about the jeep?" He shook his head as he watched the sweat beads pop to Ches's forehead and Ches grit his teeth. "Man, that has'ta hurt..."

Before he could finish his sentence, Ches had him snagged within his webbing and reeled in like a fish.

"Geesh, Ches, at least give me some warning..."

Suddenly, Ches bolted off the edge of the cliff and dove toward the trees 1,000 feet below.

Trey was yanked from the edge of the cliff;

and, the cocoon he was encased in was tossed through the air like a tetherball. "Hhholyyy shiiittt!" he screamed as the ground rushed toward him with each passing second and the air was ripped from his lungs.

"Chhhessss!!!!" Suddenly, he was sucked to Ches's thorax. It was like being drawn to a gigantic magnet. Webbing darted in every direction, attaching to anything that protruded from the mountainside as they raced to the base of the mountain and the road below.

"Oh my god! You're tryin' to kill me!" Eight eyes briefly shot Trey's way; then cut in the direction of the trees and ground rushing toward them at split-second intervals.

"Dooo sommeethiinngg!!!" Trey screamed. The eight eyes again darted his way out of annoyance, then turned toward the ground rapidly racing toward them.

Without missing a beat, jets of webbing shot toward the monstrous firs and pines, latching onto anything grounded. After several seconds, Ches hit the forest floor with a thud. The commotion sent birds and wildlife scattering for cover.

They had reached the bottom of the mountain in less than twelve seconds. Trey's scattered brain had somehow mentally counted them.

"Are you crazy?" he shouted at Ches. His body was trembling and his heart banged against his back and ribs.

Ches's eight eyes shot his way, followed by his large fangs. A low hissing sound reverberated deep within Ches's throat as he released a warm breath of air upon Trey's face.

"Now, Ches..."

As suddenly as the fangs had appeared, they disappeared; and, Ches bolted toward the river and Bear Mountain.

# Chapter 13

**Lana** groaned as she blinked her eyes then slowly opened them to the dim lighting coming from an overhead fluorescent light where she was being held in the back of the truck. Pain shot through her skull as she attempted to sit up and focus; however, she couldn't. While she was sedated, they had placed a large, steel inlayed net across her and bolted it down, and she had transformed back to her human state. The netting felt rough to her skin and was extremely heavy. She would never escape.

"Oh my god!" she shrieked as her senses abruptly cleared and her sights settled on a soldier sitting on a crate cattycorner to her. Quickly, she commanded her webbing to stream around the crucial parts of her bare body then along her legs and torso. It was cold in the truck. Not only would the webbing cover the parts she didn't want anyone else to see, but it would also help to keep her warm.

The soldier stared at her, watched her like a hawk observing its prey. His weapon's safety was off, just waiting for any sign that she was trying to escape.

A brief smile crested his lips as he swirled his tongue around a paperclip that hung from the corner of his mouth and his eyes sparked with a hunger—a hunger to pull the trigger and kill.

Evan? She wanted to cry out his name, call for him to see if he was okay. She knew he was in the van behind them. His heartbeat was low and steady and his temperature remained cool; he was heavily sedated. Diana was with him. Her heart pounded angrily within her chest and her blood boiled beneath her skin.

Lana's mind raced to the promise she and Evan had made to one another—a promise as husband and wife. Quickly, she glanced at her hand which was tucked beneath her cheek. The ring was gone; she had lost it when she had transformed.

Tears burst at the back of her eyes and she couldn't help but cry.

The soldier just sat there and watched her.

**The** vehicles containing Evan and Lana were being followed by a third which carried several soldiers from Brant military base. Racing along the long, mud-covered road, they made their way into the mountains. The heavy rains had played havoc with the land, gouging out large chunks of road and filling the small riverbeds, rushing creeks and overbearing rivers.

Suddenly, Lana heard someone yell, "Hold up!" Then, the truck she was in came to a screeching halt. Several other soldiers' voices sounded outside along with a knock on the side of the truck.

"Hey Tony, are you okay in there?"

A twinkle collected in the soldier's eyes as

he stood and glanced at Lana lying on the floor. Then, removing the paperclip from the corner of his mouth he shouted back, "Sure. No problems here."

"Is the creature awake?"

"Yep," he responded. "She's human now."

"I'm gonna' send in Fred and Mackie."

"Sounds good ta' me," Tony replied. Then, he asked, "So, why'd we stop?"

The soldier outside the truck responded, "The road's been washed out. We're gonna' have'ta double back around or construct a small bridge. I'll let ya' know what's happening in a few minutes."

Tony sat back down and looked at Lana. Their eyes locked.

"Don't get any ideas." He patted his gun. "After what you did to Corporal Anderson, you make one false move and I'll blow you from here to Mars." His tongue quickly appeared again and rolled around the paperclip which was now between his lips.

Lana quickly averted her gaze and rubbed her eyes with the back of her trembling hand. Then, she quickly curled into a fetal position as the back of the truck was opened and two soldiers jumped in. The doors were immediately closed behind them. The two soldiers' eyes locked on her as they found a seat on one of the several crates bolted to the floor.

"Hey, Fred...Mackie." Tony nonchalantly imitated a salute. Then, quickly removing the paperclip from his mouth, he slipped it into his breast pocket and asked, "So, what's goin' on out there?"

Mackie, who was slightly taller than the other two and looked to be in his early twenties, responded, "The damn road's been washed away. So, we volunteered to come back here and help you out."

Tony nodded his head in Lana's direction. "Do I look like I need help? Look at her." All eyes shifted in Lana's direction. "After she transformed back to her human state, she started bawlin' and hasn't stopped."

"So, this puny girl killed the corporal," the soldier named Fred, remarked as he shook his head. "Unbelievable."

"Yep. That was somethin'," Tony replied.

"Man, she's nothing more than a high school kid," Mackie noted. "It's hard to believe she killed Corporal Anderson the way she did."

Tony poked Lana in the chest with the nose of his rifle. "I think we should just kill her now while she's weak. 'An eye for an eye,' I always say."

Lana winced in pain with each jab as he poked at her chest then worked his way to her stomach. She tried desperately to control the beast that wanted to come alive and kill this person, rip him to shreds.

"Stop!" The involuntary cry suddenly slipped from her lips.

Mackie stood to his feet and positioned himself between Tony and Lana. "What's the matter with you, man? She's just a kid."

Tony shot to his feet while his few moments of fun had been interrupted by this newcomer who had only been assigned to Brant a week ago. Anger thundered across his chiseled, olive-colored features. "Stand down, soldier," he spewed. "That thing just killed a U.S. commander."

Sparks raced in every direction as the two men, their fingers itchy on their triggers, eyed each other closely.

"Hold on, you two," Fred quickly stepped between them. "No one's killing any thing or any body." His menacing look held them both at bay. "Besides, if we do anything to jeopardize this mission, Brant will have all our hides. They demanded the subjects be delivered alive. So, if that means I have to report you both to keep them living, I will."

"Ya' know, Fred..." Tony's brows met, "...you may be our superior, but if it came to kicking ass, I'd give ya' a real run for your money."

Fred's wrinkled lips curled. "Go ahead and try me, boy."

Mackie stepped in behind Tony.

Tony's gaze cut between the two, knowing he was outmanned. "Maybe another time." He shot an icy stare in Lana's direction and then sat down.

Mackie turned his attention to Lana; then, removing his vest, he covered her with it. Lana looked up at him through large teary eyes.

"Thank you."

Mackie lightly smiled. "You're welcome."

"Shit," Tony muttered. "Ya' gonna coddle her too?"

Ignoring his remark, Mackie sat down, laid

117

his head back, and briefly closed his eyes. Fred sat down beside him and watched Tony carefully.

## Pinkerton's Store

**Lucinda** pulled up in front of Pinkerton's Store and parked.

"Just let it run, dear," Jacob told her. "I'll only be a minute." Quickly opening the passenger door, he headed inside.

They had canvassed the area asking several of the locals if they knew who might own the vehicle Jacob described to them. Some of the folk had mentioned that they thought it belonged to Trey Yanney. In fact, the name had come up several times.

Jacob had Lucinda pull into the local corner store. It had been awhile since they had left home and, with Lucinda being pregnant, he needed to get her something to drink; plus, he wanted to ask the clerk if they knew anything about Trey.

The tiny bells over the door rang and the attendant quickly appeared from the backroom.

"Good afternoon," the gentlemen stated kindly.

"Good afternoon," Jacob responded impassively. Glancing in the large cooler displaying milk and juice and a variety of other drinks, he opened the door and selected water and an apple juice.

The gentleman busied himself with straightening the various sizes of cups for the soda fountain and quickly wiping its messed counter. Then, he hurried behind the cash register as Jacob placed his drinks on the counter before the man.

"Will there be anything else?" the man asked. His rushing around had produced tiny beads of sweat upon his forehead. Pushing his thick framed glasses back, he ran a sleeve across his face.

Jacob eyed him briefly, then replied, "I would like to ask you a few questions."

The man looked up at Jacob; and, his face suddenly looked like he had stepped out of a sauna. A mild tremble resounded in his reply, "I guess."

"Do you know a Trey Yanney who drives a black charger with the license plate, H-R-D-A-S-S? Someone told me he stops in here quite frequently."

"Well...yes," the man slightly stammered. "I know Trey. Has he done something wrong?"

The corners of Jacob's mouth turned up slightly. "Oh, no. See, my wife and he are cousins." He pointed to his car sitting outside. "She's in the car now. She's expecting our third child."

"Oh, that's nice." The man quickly nodded his head.

Jacob averted his gaze to the drinks still sitting on the counter.

"Oh, I'm sorry about that." Rapidly spinning on his heels, the man immediately began to ring up the apple juice and water; then, he hurriedly placed them in a brown paper bag.

"Anyway," Jacob continued. "She—my wife—hasn't seen Trey in a long time and she would like to go visit and tell him about the new baby."

"Well, in that case," the man stated, "Trey

lives about fifteen, sixteen miles from here. But, you aren't gonna' catch him at home. He and Ches Starling just stopped in for supplies about two hours ago. They're headed up to their cabin in the mountains."

"Does Ches Starling have dark hair?" Jacob recalled the fight Evan was engaged in. His opponent, another black widow male, had sun bleached blonde hair.

"Oh, no," the man chuckled. "He's blonde like a surfer boy; drives a black jeep."

Jacob thought a moment. "And, the cabin's in Bear Mountain?"

"Oh, no. It's located just beyond Mercy Park." Pushing back his glasses and avoiding Jacob's insistent stare, the man asked, "Are ya' familiar with it?"

"Yes, I am," Jacob responded. "I did some hunting up there a few years back."

"Oh." The man then handed Jacob his bag. "That'll be $3.65."

Jacob pulled a five dollar bill from his pocket and handed it to the man. "Keep the change."

Smiling, the man nodded his head. "Thank you." Relieved, he watched as Jacob exited the store. Then, suddenly, he scowled and scratched the side of his neck.

"He hunted up there a few years back?" he spoke aloud. "That's odd. No one's been allowed to hunt up there for the past forty years; and, that young fella' looks to be no older than twenty five."

Still pondering Jacob's comment, the man returned to his chore of arranging the soda fountain cups and wiping down the counters.

**Jacob** opened the car door and climbed in.

"So, did you find anything out?" Lucinda's low voice was plagued with anxiety.

"Yes, I did," he answered as he held the brown bag open for her to choose one of the refreshments. She chose the apple juice. Then, quickly uncapping the water, he took a drink. I want you to drive north, to the outskirts of town, and drop me off."

"What's out there?"

"Ches Starling—our other black widow."

# Chapter 14

**The** rain had stopped; however, the heavy layer of dark clouds, that had begun to disperse, regrouped and remained overhead.

Ches raced along the forest floor then sailed through the air clearing 100 feet with each hurdle. His adrenaline soared, causing his arachnid awareness and abilities to heighten. Lana, his human thoughts raced nearly as fast as his black widow senses, I'll be there as soon as I can.

"Ches," Trey yelled, "Do you know where they are?" Two large eyes turned his way and briefly watched him; then, they averted back to the forest and mountain terrain before them.

"I guess that means yes," Trey muttered to himself.

Within minutes, they had cleared thirty miles which would have taken them nearly an hour if they would have driven the jeep. Bear Mountain was just ahead.

Suddenly, Ches veered right and landed on a huge branch high up in the trees. His fangs rapidly appeared and a low hiss reverberated in his open throat.

"What is it?" Trey shielded his eyes and gazed out into the forest. The vegetation was too thick and they were up too high; he couldn't see a thing. However, as he listened closely, he could hear what sounded like hammering in the distance.

"What is that?" he lowly spoke. He noticed the billions of tiny hairs on Ches's arachnid form were perked to attention, concentrating on something in the near distance.

Suddenly, Ches scurried to another branch; then, as webbing shot from his spinneret, he glided to the ground. Trey was quickly released with a swipe of Ches's leg which tore through the strands of the cocoon.

"Whatrya doing?" Trey scowled. "I'm coming with you." The large eyes just stared back at him. "Geez, I don't know if you can understand me or not." He tried again; this time in a slow motion monologue along with several hand gestures. "I...want...to...come...with...you." There was no response.

"Geez, Ches—you need to tap one of those ugly feet or nod your head. Do something besides just stand there and look at me with those big goofy eyeballs of yours. You're creepin' me out." Ches's fangs appeared and he hissed.

Taking a step back and nervously grinning, Trey pointed a finger at him. "See, now that's a start. I know that means you're pissed off."

Ches moved toward him, his fangs beginning to drip with venom. Trey's voice mildly shook. "Hey, now what are you trying to say? I hope it's not that you're hungry. Remember what you said, Ches: You didn't think I'd taste very good. And, I had a spinach omelet for breakfast. You know how much you hate spinach." Ches took another step, then suddenly he sprang.

"Gah!" Trey flinched as Ches charged toward him. Then, to his surprise, bound past him and disappeared.

Stunned, Trey gazed in the direction of where Ches had gone. The unsettled brush and trees still slightly shivered; then, they came to a stop.

"Hey!" he hollered to the emptiness. "I told you I wanted to go with you!" He glanced around at his surroundings and added, "Besides—I don't know where the hell I am!"

**Ches** hurriedly made his way toward the military truck where Lana was being held. The three vehicles were sitting along the old mountain pass which led up the side of Bear Mountain where the road sat about 400 feet high on an outcropping of the ridge. One false move and the entire entourage would be plummeting to the base of the mountain.

The main road was washed out. Several men were busying themselves in the attempt to construct a makeshift bridge for the vehicles to pass over, while three others, who were blocked from view by the truck holding Lana, were digging notches in the side of the mountain. Another six were toiling away at cutting down small trees and fastening them together with rope. And, with the few others that moved about the area, there were fourteen in all. Ches could sense Jacob nearby, ready to make his move; and, Evan, Lana and

Diana were inside the vehicles.

Ches moved swiftly, quietly, settling himself within a tree just feet from where the military motorcade was. His desire to free Lana was driving his inner beast crazy. He would need to strike quickly, effectively, and without alerting the entire assemblage of men which would endanger her. And, he would only kill if absolutely necessary. Without making a sound, he struck.

Webbing shot in the three men's direction and he quickly encased them to their upper lips. The others hadn't noticed. So, snatching them one at a time from their appointed spots, he dragged them toward where he was.

Next, he concentrated on the six men who were scattered in various spots within the trees: This would be more difficult, especially since they were all heavily armed. All he needed to do was get to the vehicle where Lana was. Quietly, he raced toward the truck as Jacob appeared within the trees; he was getting in a better position.

Suddenly, the driver's door popped open. The solder's head spun as he did a double-take at the sight of Ches charging in their direction.

"Holy shit!" The driver hurriedly pulled his weapon. "One of the spiders is loose!"

The passenger door flew open and the other man got out. "It's not ours. It must be the kid in the van. Alert the others!" Drawing his gun, he crouched down and raced around the side of the truck.

**Diana** irritably tapped her foot against the

cold floor of the van. Her pajamas and hair had finally dried; however, despite the heated anger that raged inside her, she was shivering.

"Ya'll could at least turn some heat on back here," she groaned. Then, shifting in her seat, she attempted to look out the windshield. The men were shouting and scattering like bugs. Something was going on. Quickly, she glanced at Evan to see if he had stirred.

Nothing.

Suddenly, the van was slammed from behind and the impact buckled the rear of the vehicle. It sent Diana jerking at her restraints. "Ow!" she cried as she attempted to sit upright in her seat. Suddenly, they were slammed again and the van was tipping on its side. Diana screamed.

"Help!" The sound of her own screaming rang in her ears as she tried to hang on. "Evan! Wake up! Evan..."

It was Ches. He had wrapped the driver of the truck inside his cocoon. However, he was suddenly rammed from behind as the last truck bolted forward and drove him into the back of the van.

Screeching in anger, he spun and charged. The truck bolted forward again and slammed him into the van again.

**An** eerie blackness surrounded Evan as he lay in a coma-like sleep. In some ways, he wished he'd never wake up.

Lana...he silently called out her name. She was no where in the blackness; it was only him and an abrupt screaming that kept ringing in his ears.

Who's screaming, he wearily pondered—screaming and disturbing my restful slumber? Pain shot through his wrists and ankles like spikes being driven through his flesh. Where had he seen that being performed before, known of its cruel existence? His thoughts were churning like fruit in a blender—some pieces large as life, while others were puréed to oblivion.

Suddenly, his body slammed against something cold and hard and he was forced to open his eyes. He was being tossed about like a rag doll, yanked against the shackles that held him in place.

The restraints tore at his wrists and ankles and he yanked at the metal chains. "Shit!" He was trying to get his bearings; however, the rolling van made it nearly impossible. And, the screaming that continued to tear at his eardrums, caused his clouded mind to want to shrivel up and die.

Then, without warning, his arachnid burst to life and ripped through his skin. The change came quickly. And, as his form grew larger, his body pushed through the broken windshield of the van and partially out the open doors. His upper torso remained trapped inside, while his lower body was being compressed by the crushed metal of the front end.

A screech tore from his throat as he struggled to break free and stop the vehicle from rolling. However, being partially trapped and still heavily drugged, he was unable to get his bearings and use his webbing.

Blonde hair whipped before him; and, his

arachnid, irritated by Diana's shrill assailant of shrieks, bore its fangs. He would bite her. Shut her up.

A growl tore from Evan's throat; and, with the appearance of his fangs, droplets of venom flew in every direction.

The van continued to roll. Then, suddenly, without warning, the vehicle groaned and came to a halt.

Diana's tear-filled eyes were wide as saucers as she looked at Evan's beastly form just inches from her face. Her heart banged within her ears and her entire body trembled. She gripped at the shackles holding her in place, preparing for the vehicle to roll again. Her voice shook and she could barely say his name. "Evan?"

He was wedged between the motor and the front seats and he needed to break free— not only from the vehicle that was rapidly being crushed, but also from Diana's screaming which had scraped against his every nerve.

Briefly, his eight eyes stared at her, tried to figure out how to quiet the nuisance. A low hiss slipped from behind his exposed fangs and he abruptly bit though her shackles to break her free, free so she could get as far away from him as possible.

Evan shifted his weight and the van began to roll again.

# Chapter 15

    **A** hailstorm of bullets rained upon Jacob as he made his move and the other soldiers responded. Dodging the onslaught, he raced past Ches who was determined not to be run over or crushed by the truck.

    Jacob was attempting to reach the van before it was flattened to a doormat. His concern wasn't so much with Evan; but, with the female who was trapped inside. Evan had a better chance at surviving the fall; however, she didn't.

    His spinneret blasted webbing in every direction which clung to anything that was grounded. And, sailing through the air, he landed just above the van which was beginning to pick up speed in its descent downhill. Webbing coated everything in sight, including the vehicle. This slowed its fall somewhat and for a brief moment brought it to a halt. However, the next drop would send it plummeting down a 300 foot cliff. Jacob had just seconds to get Evan and Diana out.

    A torrent of silver strands suddenly shot through the air and latched onto the van along with Jacob's webbing. It was Ches. He had encased the entire truck-full of soldiers in a massive cocoon which would only hold them for a few moments. Then, he spun to assist with Evan and Diana's rescue, not to reach Evan and save him, but to beat Evan to a pulp. This was the last time Evan was putting Lana in danger. Ches would make certain of that.

Instinctively, Jacob's fangs appeared at the presence of Ches and he released a low hiss. Briefly, a staring match ensued. Then, suddenly, their attention was drawn as Jacob's webbing snapped and the van began to roll again.

Diana's screaming reverberated along the mountain side as the vehicle disappeared over the 300 foot drop.

Jacob raced toward the cliff's edge to see Evan's large black widow form hanging over the side. Diana was caught in his webbing, dangling upside down by her foot.

"Oh my god! Help me!!" She screamed while her arms thrashed about wildly as if she were flying or attempting to paddle through water. It seemed to Jacob as if she was swimming in a high speed competition and, her screaming and flailing of arms would increase her speed.

Quickly targeting Diana, Jacob aimed for her with his webbing. His aim was right on, perfected by his intense practice and utilization at home while he had always made it a point to be ready to protect his family.

Immediately, he had Diana snagged within the sturdy strands and yanked toward him. He watched her as she slipped to the ground and blubbered a few indiscernible words. She looked to him for comfort; but, he wasn't giving any. She was lucky he had even saved her—he could care less about anyone else. His family was all that mattered.

Briefly, he observed her. Terror was ignited as a fiery flame in her eyes; and, her swollen, trembling cheeks twisted unnaturally as she continued to cry. Blood ran from a gash in her hair; he thought she may be going into shock.

Suddenly, her head dropped within her hands. Momentarily, he listened to her cries, then he was off in the direction of the soldiers and the fight that was taking place.

**Evan**, still in his arachnid form, arduously climbed up over the edge of the cliff and shook his head in the attempt to gather his senses. Something, besides Diana's crying abruptly caught his attention. It caused the billions of tiny hairs lining his form to grasp at the slight breeze that was wafting along his body.

Throwing his head in the air, he remained absolutely still. Something had changed—something with Lana. He was also aware of Ches's presence.

His black eyes blazed with fury as a low shrieking rose from his throat and his gaze shot up the hill to the truck where she was.

Two of his legs were injured badly; he would need time to heal. However, that time wasn't now. Right now, he needed to get to Lana.

Immediately, he charged in her direction.

**The** moment Evan had crested the ridge, Ches was bombarded with Lana's scent which was imbedded in Evan's black widow body and shell. It was overwhelming and saturating, flooding Ches's senses like a heavy perfume. Evan had basked in Lana's female scent—had made himself her mate. He had defiled her.

"Evan!" Ches bellowed from within his human self, "What have you done? I'll kill you!" His teeth chattered as he screeched in rage and his fangs dripped with venom. Within seconds, he spanned the distance between them and slammed Evan to the ground.

The fight would be to the death.

Using his legs like sharpened blades, he sliced at Evan's arachnid body. Then, blasting him with a mass amount of webbing, Ches speedily began to wrap Evan in an airtight cocoon.

"Stop!" Diana screamed through teary eyes. "Stop fighting!"

Jacob spun and watched from a distance, realizing this was the male arachnid's battle for a female. He needed to stay out of it; however, he couldn't ignore the fact that the webbing Ches had secured the soldiers in wouldn't last forever. They had already begun to cut through it and would be out any moment.

**Trey** ran toward the gunfire, then toward the screaming and crunching of metal that echoed throughout the valley. It was Diana; he could recognize her southern twang anywhere.

"Ches, I'll never forgive you for this." He quickly bent to take a breath. "I'll be dead, before I get to ya'."

An eerie torrent of screeches reverberated through the trees, sending a spiky sensation racing along his spine. Shifting the bundled rope, he stood up and began running again.

**"Evan!"** Ches was unable to control the rage that was blazing inside him. The thought of Lana being defiled was nauseating, almost too much to bear. Evan had broken the gentleman's rule. No, he had broken every rule.

Bearing his fangs, he tore into the cocoon and plunged them deep within Evan's exoskeleton.

Evan shrieked and bucked against the explosion of pain. His injuries and the effects of the tranquilizer were making it nearly impossible for him to break free of the thick layer of webbing Ches had trapped him in.

Ches! You're finished! I don't care how mad Lana gets! I went easy on you in the past. The words seethed in his mind as he fought arduously to tear through the cocoon. However, when I get outta here, you're dead!

**Lana** lifted her head to the horrifying sounds she was hearing outside the truck. The soldiers inside the vehicle with her were tense, their weapons ready to fire.

"Evan—Ches..." She could sense they were both nearby and in their arachnid form.

"Whaddaya think's going on out there?" Mackie's wide eyes met the gaze of his superior, Fred.

Without replying, Fred pulled his two-way

radio from his belt. "Unit 2, what the hell's going on out there?"

The silence was nerve-racking until static filled the small speaker. Then, there was a rushed, unclear response.

"It's the spiders! We've been attacked; and, they're on the loose!"

Fred's throat suddenly became tight, restricted; he swallowed hard and barked into the radio, "Soldier, get a grip on yourself!" His aged hand held the radio tighter. "How many are there?"

"Three. Three that we've seen so far."

"And, where is your commanding officer?" Fred asked.

There was a moment of silence then the voice responded, "DOA, sir. He was suffocated by their webbing."

"Shit!" Tony stared wildly at Fred. "I told you we should've just killed 'em! Now, those bastards have gone and killed another one of ours!"

Tony immediately spun and his booted heel thumped upon Lana's chest. And, quickly releasing the safety on his weapon, he stuck the end of it in her face.

"Well, if any of them are males, this one is our meal ticket."

Lana's eyes bulged with fear.

"Hold on, Tony," Mackie stepped toward him.

Without warning, Tony swung his rifle, making contact with Mackie's face. A sickening crack sounded in the younger soldier's chin as his head snapped back and his eyes shot up into his head. His limp body crashed to the truck floor.

"Private!" Fred shouted. "Stand down!"

The nose of Tony's weapon swung in Fred's direction. "No! You stand down, old man. I'll be damned if I'm gonna' let some huge spider eat or suffocate me!" He grabbed the radio from Fred's hand; then, he grabbed Fred's sidearm. "Now, get over in that corner, before I put a bullet in your chest."

Tony then yelled into the radio, "Jeremy, get Nicolas and whoever's left and meet me at the back of the cargo truck. And, bring plenty of ammo. I'm gettin' us outta' here."

"Roger that," Jeremy replied.

Lana watched as Tony removed some rope from inside one of the crates and secured Fred's arms and legs, then bound his mouth. She flinched as Tony grabbed her foot, unlatched the iron shackle, then did the same to her other foot and her wrists. Grabbing her, he tied her hands and feet, then jerked her to standing.

"Come on, you're our ticket outta' here," he growled.

"Please, don't do this." Lana stumbled forward, as Tony opened the rear doors to the truck, and nearly dragged her out the back. The barrel of his gun jabbed at her side. "Evan will kill you."

"Oh, shut up!" Tony hollered in her ear.

Feeling as if her eardrum had been busted, Lana winced in pain.

# Chapter 16

**"Stop it!"** Diana screamed again. "Quit fighting!"

Ches's fangs plunged into Evan once more sending Evan's black widow form arching in excruciating pain.

Ches angrily tossed Evan. Then, bounding upon him with the force of a rhino, he drove Evan into the muddy earth. "I'll tear you to shreds, make you pay for what you did!" his human thoughts shouted.

Evan's massive body lay in a puddle of bloody water. Ches had injured him badly. One more strike with Ches's poisonous fangs and he would be finished.

Then, as if Ches had been struck, his head shot up and for a brief moment, he stood absolutely still. A sharp, familiar scent ran through the tiny hairs covering his body and alerting his senses. His eight eyes darted toward the two vehicles sitting above them along the mountainside. It was Lana; she was being moved from out of the truck.

Momentarily, his gaze cut to Evan and a loud screech tore from his throat. I'll finish you off later! The thought blasted through his mind. Then, within seconds, he was scaling the side of the mountain and racing toward Lana. Jacob was just ahead of him.

The remaining seven soldiers who hadn't been suffocated by Ches's webbing stood with their firearms ready, in formation, behind the truck.

Tony jumped down onto the muddy ground and immediately yanked Lana down onto his shoulder. Hurriedly, he shouted to Jeremy and Nicolas, a large black soldier. "Jeremy, Nicolas— what do we know about the three arachnids?"

Jeremy quickly responded. "Well, the one is Evan Labonte who we detained earlier. And, the other two, we're not sure. However, we do know one thing—all three are males. They have the markings of males. In fact, two have been fighting."

"Good," Tony remarked. "If they're males maybe they'll kill each other."

"Well, I wouldn't be too sure about that," Nicolas stated. "Norris spotted two heading up the side of the mountain; they'll be here any second."

Tony growled as his dark brows met. "Then, what are we standing around for? Get in position; and, as soon as they crest the ridge, fire!"

**Evan** began the laborious task of biting through the cocoon, within minutes he was free. His strength was gone, used to escape the van and fight off Ches. He was mud covered and bleeding; however, he had to help Lana. He needed to feed.

Briefly, he glanced at Diana—she would more than feed his warranted appetite. However, he abhorred the idea of feasting on anything living, especially a human.    There had to be something nearby. His black widow required the nourishment for survival. Spying two possums that sat still as statues in the cover of the nearby weeds, he lunged. He would be certain to make their deaths quick, while he hated the thought of anyone or anything suffering. Obtaining the life source he needed, he painstakingly made his way up the mountainside.

"Evan, look out! It's an ambush!" he could hear Lana cry.

"Shut up, you!" a voice snapped.

Ches suddenly sprung into the air followed by Jacob. Gunfire sprayed the area as their webbing coated everything in sight.

"Hold your ground, men!" Tony barked as he speedily dodged the strands that had already snagged three men.

Nicolas's booming voice shouted "Fire in the hole!" as he hurriedly tossed a grenade at Ches and Jacob and the men ran for cover. Tony and Jeremy slipped around the back of the truck and hit the mud-covered earth. The ground shook and Lana screamed at the blast that shot through her head. The pain was excruciating, unbearable and her two hands gripped at her ears.

"Oh my god! Oh my god!"

"Shut up!" Tony shouted as he hastily climbed to his feet and yanked her back onto his shoulder.

Suddenly, another explosion sent them crashing to the muddy earth. Lana continued to scream.

The few remaining men scattered in every direction as Ches angrily bounded atop the truck. His eight eyes cut through the flying rubble to Lana being held on the ground. Fury blazed in his stare, and the beast he had become wanted to kill, maim anyone involved with her abduction. However, he was caught off guard as the truck rocked and buckled and Evan suddenly leapt onto the vehicle behind him. Rapidly spinning, he braced himself as Evan charged toward him with the force of a steam roller.

Tony and Jeremy moved quickly, taking cover within the nearby trees.

"What about Nicolas and the others?" Jeremy asked.

Tony's eyes glinted maniacally as his forearm tightened around Lana and his hand gripped at his firearm. "They're on their own."

Jeremy nodded his head and briefly watched the two black widows fighting. The truck was buckling beneath their large body masses and weakening the already unstable ground.

"Evan! Stop!" Lana suddenly yelled out. "There are men in that truck. You'll kill them!"

"Be quiet!" Tony hissed as he quickly crouched down. Evan and Ches's attention shot in their direction. In a blink of an eye, Evan was flying through the air and crashing through the trees.

"Holy shit!" Jeremy's gunfire sprayed the area with gunshot, like a swarm of angry hornets.

Ches, joining the fight, blasted Jeremy with webbing. In a matter of seconds, Jeremy was completely encased.

"Tony!" Jeremy screamed in terror. "Get me outta' here!"

Tony jumped to his feet; and, grabbing Lana by the hair, he shoved his gun to her cheek. "Let him go or I'll kill her!"

Ches immediately released Jeremy and stepped back.

Evan screeched in rage as hatred blazed in his eyes. His beast was assessing the situation, placing each remaining man and beast. With the exception of Jacob and Lana, he was surrounded by the opposition.

The area suddenly became still except for the several grunts coming from Nicolas who was struggling to get out from beneath Jacob and the hastened breaths and footfalls of the soldiers who were encircling them.

"Back off!" Tony shouted as he sprayed the air with gunfire, "You're surrounded!" The nose of his heated gun then again played at Lana's cheek; the cold metal tore through her skin.

Evan's stare cut to Ches as Ches's vital signs sky-rocketed and Ches stepped forward.

"I mean it!" Tony's wild gaze darted between the two. "Back away!" Then, he shouted to Jeremy and Nicolas, "Get the men in the last truck."

Brant Military Base was another two miles north. He and the men needed to get there—there they could get the assistance they needed.

Slowly, they backed to the rear of the vehicle and one by one disappeared inside. Tony was the last to move as he yanked Lana in that direction.

**Evan** stood as a statue. His gaze shot between Tony's itchy trigger finger, Ches, and Lana who stared at him in terror. The black widow within him was ready to snap, tear this individual apart who was using Lana as a human shield. Unable to control the beast any longer, he sprung.

Tony whipped in Evan's direction and discharged a swarm of bullets. The men in the truck immediately appeared and also began to fire. Evan dodged, however, was unable to avoid the onslaught.

"Evan!" Lana screamed as Evan took several bullets to the chest and head. And, though he was badly injured, he was tearing through the men with a vengeance.

Lana's body shook as she suddenly transformed. And, within seconds, her fangs were clinging to Tony's neck.

**In** a combined effort, Jacob and Ches charged the other men. They quickly encased them in a heavily layered cocoon—one they wouldn't escape from for hours. Then, they watched as Lana transformed back to her human form and quickly went to Evan's side. He was sitting on the ground in his human form, his injuries slowly healing.

"Evan...are you okay?" She gently touched his face.

"Yeah," he wearily responded. "Just give me a minute."

Lana wrapped her arms around his neck. "I

was so worried about you."

Ches quickly transformed and angrily pushed past her. Rage burned in his icy glare.

"I should kill you, Evan!"

Evan's cold stare shifted upward. "If you wanna' address me, wrap yourself or get some clothes on. I certainly don't wanna' look at you; and, I don't want Lana looking at you either."

Crimson brushed along Lana's cheeks, while she was glad she had perfected the use of her webbing to cover her body. Though, Ches and Evan didn't seem bothered by their nudity, being naked after transforming was embarrassing; and, seeing them naked was even more mortifying.

Ches's fists curled and his tone was as stone. "Well, she surely doesn't need to be looking at you either; though, I know you've forced yourself upon her and made her look at you."

"What do you mean—forced myself upon her and made her look at me?" Evan wobbled to his feet. "Did you get hit in the head with somethin', Ches? I don't recall you being tossed around the back of the van and nearly getting your head smashed in!"

Ches's right fist suddenly made contact with Evan's jaw.

# Chapter 17

**"Ches!** Stop!" Lana grabbed his arm. "What are you talking about? Evan didn't force himself on me."

"Don't lie for him, Lana. His stench is all over you." He placed his hands on her shoulders, his eyes searching hers. "I know what he did."

"He didn't do anything, Ches."

"What are you trying to say?" Disbelief rang in his voice. "Are you trying to say that you let him—that you let him touch you?"

Lowering her head, she softly replied, "Yes, Ches, I did." She briefly paused then added. "He's my husband and I'm his wife."

Horror struck him like an iron fist nearly knocking him backward. "His wife? When did that happen?"

"Last night," she stated quietly. "We made a promise..."

"A promise? You became husband and wife on a promise? Did he even propose or anything before he..." He agitatedly ran a hand through his hair. The words blurted from his mouth. "Before he violated you!"

Sadness filled Lana's eyes. "He didn't violate me, Ches. And, yes, he did propose and he gave me a ring. But, I lost it."

Quickly, she turned to Evan, tears breaking at the back of her lids. "I'm so sorry. I lost your ring when I transformed back at the cabin. I'm really sorry."

Regret briefly shadowed Evan's gaze, then he replied, "Its okay. I guess that just means I'll have to get you another one sooner than we thought."

"Oh, no..." Lana paused. "I don't want another ring..."

Jacob, transformed to his human state, suddenly interrupted their conversation. Lana's crimson cheeks burned bright red as she immediately turned her head, trying to avoid looking at him.

"Look, Evan—we don't have time for this. Those men won't stay bound forever. And, if we're going to get her brother out of Brant, we should do it now—without this childish nonsense."

Jacob's dark gaze then brushed over Evan and settled on Ches. A staring matched ensued; then, Jacob stated, "Thank you for the help."

Ches's azure colored eyes narrowed as he spoke. "I'm only here for Lana—to protect her."

"Well, again, thank you for your assistance. However, your presence is causing a problem, so you'll need to leave."

"Why should I leave?" The cords in Ches's neck abruptly popped.

"Because, apparently, this female is not interested in you being her mate. This female has chosen someone else."

"And, who are you to judge?" Ches yelled. Anger and hurt boiled beneath his skin. Suddenly he swung; however, Jacob was quick and caught his fist midair.

Jacob's breath was hot upon Ches's face and his tone was marked. Blackness covered his stare. "Don't even try me. Or, it'll be the last thing you do." He shoved Ches's fist away.

Ches glanced over at Lana. He seemed to be buckling inside. "Is this what you want, Lana? Do you want me to leave—leave you alone?"

Though the pain on Ches's face was agonizing, Lana quietly nodded her head.

"All right," he stated as he fought the pain that reared from his aching heart. Turning on his heels, he rapidly transformed. Then, releasing a long, heartrending screech, he took off in the direction from which he had come earlier.


**Diana** watched as Lana, Evan and Jacob metamorphosed into the dark creatures that were the other side of them. And, hearing every word they had said, she slowly slumped against a nearby tree.


**Trey** caught his breath as a squeak slipped from his quavering lips. "Ches?" The woods in the distance cracked and splintered while birds and wildlife scrambled for cover. Something was charging through the forest, something big and something powerful.

Quickly, he hid behind the trunk of a large maple while sweat beaded the back of his neck and each passing second was torture. Frantically, he searched the buckling and snapping trees, waiting for whatever it was.

All of a sudden, a huge black widow spider burst through the trees. It was covering the ground at top speed; and, it was charging toward him.

"Holy crap!" Trey crowed as he sprung backward and did a one eighty to get away. Suddenly, it swerved and ran past him. Then, within a blink of an eye, it was gone. Something told Trey it was Ches.

"Ches!" he shouted, "Ches, wait!"

Trey dropped to his knees and grabbed his head with both hands. "Ugh!" Being completely exhausted, he rolled over onto his side and lay on the ground for a moment. This is a problem, he surmised. He didn't know where he was and what he should do next; plus, he was hungry.

"Oh great."

Unsure as to how long he had laid there, he allowed his body to rest and his thoughts to collect. However, at the moment, he knew two things: One—he definitely needed to find his way out of the woods before dark. And, secondly, when he caught up to Ches, he was going to, without a doubt, give him a good dose of sore ass with his size eleven boot—whether it was his own or Ches's.

Rolling onto his back, he looked up.

"Gah!" Ches was, surprisingly, standing over him. "Geez, Ches! You scared that lump of beans I ate last night right outta' me. What the hell are you doing?"

Sitting up, he quickly averted his gaze. "And gee, could ya' not stand so close; your junk is startin' ta' creep me out. Packages that big only belong under Christmas trees."

There was no reply as Ches turned and slowly began to walk away. Concentrating on his webbing, he wrapped himself in the same fashion Lana had and continued in the direction they had come. He didn't care about being naked; he didn't care about anything right now. Lana had given herself to Evan, had chosen him.

"Ches!" Trey scrambled to his feet and grabbed Ches by the shoulder. "What is going on? Why won't you answer me?"

"Get off me." Ches yanked his arm away. "We have to get back to the jeep."

"No! Now wait a minute damnit!" Trey stopped in his tracks. "You drug me all the way out here, nearly killed me in your skydiving attempt, left me in the middle of nowhere, then, nearly trampled me. And now, you won't talk to me? What the hell is up with you?"

"Just leave me alone," Ches stated lowly as he continued to walk.

"No, I won't leave you alone. What I really should do is kick your ass!" Trey suddenly jumped onto Ches's back. "You owe me an apology!"

"Get off me, you half wit!" Ches quickly threw his fist back catching Trey in the eye.

"Gah! You big lump!" Trey shouted. Swinging his fists, he caught Ches in the ear.

Ches immediately grabbed Trey's arm. His reflexes sparked and each word came as a slow, enunciated growl, "Trey...I'm...warning...you."

Trey hit him in the ear again; however, with the other fist.

"That's it!" Ches yelled. Grabbing Trey by the back of the neck, he effortlessly flung him to the ground.

"Uggh!" Trey stiffened at the immense pain in his back. "Damn you, Ches."

Ches walked toward him. "I told you to leave me alone." His voice was cold.

Suddenly, Trey drove his foot into Ches's groin.

Ches buckled over and dropped to his knees. "That was dirty," he groaned as he sucked at air while trying to keep his head from spinning and his stomach from twisting in his throat.

"I hate you, Trey," he replied as he lay on the ground and clutched at his stomach.

"Diddo, Ches. You nearly broke my back."

A round moment passed as they lay there in silence, then, Trey spoke. "I take it, all this has to do with Lana—doesn't it?"

Ches's head unexpectedly snapped in Trey's direction. Anger and hurt waged war upon his face. No longer was he calm and cool Ches Starling, Trey's very best friend; but now, he was someone or something else.

"Whaddya want me to say, Trey? Yes, it's Lana!" He was now shouting; and, his eyes were glazed as if his inner war included a battle against a malevolent army of tears.

"Is that what you wanted to hear? She's gone and married Evan. She married him last night!"

"Shit." Trey sat up and brushed a hand through his chestnut colored hair. "They got married?"

"Yeah, on some stupid promise," Ches nearly growled.

Suddenly, his balled fists hit the ground at each of his sides and he shook his head. His tone was low as he spoke.

"When Tricia died, I was devastated. I was never able to get over her, and thought for sure I'd spend the rest of my life alone."

He paused for a moment then continued, "But, then, when we found Lana, I couldn't help falling for her. For some reason, she broke through the barrier in my heart and made me feel what it's like to be loved again. Then, when we bonded through her blood, I knew I had to be with her, be a part of her. It was something about her, something that made me instantly fall in love with her. But, now that she's married..." The words burned at his innards. "I know I'll be alone forever."

Although, Trey knew it was inappropriate, he briefly succumbed to the quirky idea of them changing Diana into a black widow for Ches. Nah! Ches could never handle that type of woman— part rattler or somethin'. I can see her spewing venom now. He partially cringed then smiled inside. My kinda' woman.

Shaking his head, Trey returned his attention to Ches and chose his words carefully, "Man, there are plenty of chicks out there that wanna' be with you, especially from school."

A sarcastic look suddenly shot his way.

"Yeah right," Ches rolled his eyes. "For crying out loud, Trey, look at me!" He spread his hands before him. "I turn into something from a Peter Jackson movie, an abomination, a freak! I never planned this. After Tricia died, I just wanted to finish up school and get on with my life. But, I can't see my life going anywhere now."

"And, you're sure they got married?" Trey asked.

"That's what Lana said."

Propping himself up on an elbow, Trey rolled on his side and looked at Ches. "That's not possible if they didn't have a preacher."

"Trey, Evan has slept with her..." Briefly, he was silent. Then, the words he spoke tore at his heart as he said them. "He's impregnated her... She's going to have his child."

"Hhholllyyy shitttt!" Trey gasped as his eyes grew to saucers. "How do you know that?"

Ches closed his eyes. "I could sense the growth in her womb."

"That soon? You could sense a child that was just conceived last night, that soon?"

"Yes," Ches replied. "It's part arachnid, remember."

"Man...that really sucks. I wonder if she knows."

"I'm sure Evan does. He would have to know."

"Well...where are they now?" Trey asked.

Ches's gaze clung to the sky as he lowly spoke. "They're going to get her brother. The guy, who was there when Evan and I were brawling, is with them. He's going to help them."

"I know who you mean. That guy's creepy. He kinda' reminds me of an aristocrat Dracula."

Ches then added, "Oh, and Diana—she's here too."

"I thought that was her. What's she doing out here?"

"I don't know," Ches replied as he finally looked up. "But, she was nearly killed when she and Evan took a tumble down the side of the mountain in one of the military's vans."

"Man." Trey rubbed his chin. "I missed a lot of stuff."

"Yeah, you did," Ches answered with a heavy sigh. "I thought I would kill Evan. I knew he had been with Lana the minute I smelled her on him." Balling his large fists, he shook his head. "Man, I can't take this. Not only do I love her; but, this creature inside of me is going crazy. It's like it wants to tear through my skin and demolish everything in sight. It wants to rip Evan to pieces."

Trey groaned as he stood. Then he stepped toward Ches and laid a hand on his shoulder. "I'm sorry. This has gotta' be tough; but, I've never known you to be a quitter. We've always worked on difficult situations together and gotten through them. And, no matter what, I'm always here for ya'—whatever you need, even if you did nearly break my back when you tossed me." He wearily smiled.

"Thanks, man. You're a good friend."

"Well," Trey stated as he picked up the rope, "I know Lana cares a lot about you, even loves you; so, maybe one day she'll eat Evan after..."

Ches's head popped up; his brows narrowed over his sharp scowl as his hand shot before him. "Stop right there."

Trey shrugged theatrically, "It's just a thought." Silence briefly spanned the distance between them. Then, Trey spoke. "So whaddaya wanna do now—head back to the jeep?"

"No," Ches replied. "I don't have a good feeling about this whole thing. And, even if Lana doesn't love me and is carrying Evan's child, I have to be with her." He added, "I'll kill Evan if something happens to her. So, I'm going back."

Trey did a double-take. "Man, you sure are a glutton for punishment. If I was a chick, I'd feel lucky to have you. I think Lana's crazy for not picking you over Evan." He attempted to lighten the situation and added, "Especially, with that sweet lookin' backside you have."

Ches raised a brow. "Ya' know, Trey, after all this time, I really think you're gay."

Trey chuckled. "You'll never know will ya'."

Ches began to walk in the direction from which he had just come. "Well, after observing Lana, I can cover after transforming, and thankfully, don't have to worry about you peeking at any of my presents."

# Chapter 18

**Ches** and Trey glanced through the trees at the mess he, Evan and Jacob had left behind. The entire area was a giant mud pit with one truck crushed to the size of a mini cooper and the other vehicle dented and looking as if it had been used for target practice. The few remaining soldiers were still encased in the large cocoon he and Jacob had secured them in. Using his fangs, Jacob had punctured the webbing so they could breathe.

Briefly, it seemed odd to Ches how, as beasts, they asserted acts of kindness. Yet, on the other hand would become totally out of control. And, he had witnessed Lana killing someone and somehow it hadn't bothered him. What had they become?

The men would be free within the hour; they needed to get moving.

"Holy shit," Trey whistled low. "What a mess. You guys sure know how to throw a party."

Ches just glanced at him. This was the last thing he thought he would be doing today; and, he certainly hadn't meant for anyone to get killed. Suddenly, his senses perked up; someone was nearby. Immediately, he recognized Diana's scent.

"Diana's still here," he quietly spoke. "You

may wanna' see if she's okay."

"Diana!" Trey shouted. "Where are you? Are you okay?"

"I'm over here!" she responded from behind the trampled truck. "I need ya'lls help."

Trey and Ches hurried to see her on her hands and knees peeking through a crack in the crushed metal of the truck bed. Quickly glancing at them, she then remarked, "There's someone in here. Ya'll have'ta help him." Cuts and bruises marred her face and arms. And, her normally groomed hair was tangled, and her clothing torn.

Thinking she might be in shock, Trey hastened to her side. "Diana, are you okay?"

She looked at him strangely, as if she had no idea of who he and Ches were. Then, all of a sudden, tears burst from her eyes and she leapt into his arms.

"No, I'm not okay." Her southern accent spiked. "I was nearly killed!"

Trey stroked her disheveled hair while only catching a few of the blubbered words she was spewing.

"It's all right," he stated calmly. "You're okay now."

Moments passed as she freely wept; then, slowly, she began to collect herself. Wiping a torn sleeve of her pajamas across her eyes and nose, she blinked her red rimmed eyes. "I'm sorry."

Trey softly laughed. "What are you sorry for? You have every reason to cry."

"I know." Wearily, she smiled. Then sniffling back her tears, she stated, "I guess I was just so glad to see ya'll, I couldn't help myself. Anyway..." she pointed toward the hole in the side of the truck, "...there's someone in there; and, they can't get out. I heard them moaning a little bit ago. I'm not sure if they're still alive."

"Geez." Trey's irate stare accusingly cut to Ches. "What happened here?"

Ches just ignored him. He was concentrating more on catching Lana's scent in the mild breeze that was now wafting along his skin. He also knew there were two men in the vehicle and after helping them, he would be outta' here—on his way to see Lana. He had to; it was in his blood.

Quickly turning, he gripped the warped metal with two hands, and with all his strength he worked on prying the opening bigger.

"Grrh!" The cords on his neck, arms and chest popped as the vehicle pieces groaned and slowly succumbed to the force. The hole was only big enough for a child to crawl through. Ches peeked his head inside and looked around. It was black as pitch; however, he was able to see clearly as if someone had a light on inside.

One of the men was pinned beneath the heavy roof of the truck and one of the crates; and, the other lay unconscious on the floor: Blood lay in a small puddle at his nose. He was still alive— thank God; however, he needed medical attention. Ches thought the guy may have busted his nose when he hit the floor during he and Evan's fight. The blood smelled good.

"Hang on! I'll get you out," Ches shouted.

Brushing his arm over his sweated forehead,

Ches worked diligently at prying the metal back. After several minutes of grunts and groans from both him and the vehicle, he was able to get the hole large enough to climb inside and get the men out.

Carefully sitting one soldier on the ground, he went to retrieve the other. Trey immediately went to work on examining the unconscious soldier.

"Ches, you guys are gonna' have to be more careful." He jerked his thumb in the direction of the guy's face. "This guy has a broken jaw."

"Oh, no," Fred quickly interjected. His words sounded like he had been eating gravel. "Your friend didn't do that. That was Tony Bello—that moron. Where's that crazy bastard at anyway?" His gaze narrowed as he scanned the area. Then, leaning his head back against a piece of twisted metal of the vehicle, he inhaled deep. "Shit—who knew the day would end like this. They should have just let things alone."

"Well, maybe we should get ya'lls friend to the hospital." Diana noted as she observed from a distance.

"Don't you guys have any smelling salts or somethin' around?" Trey asked.

Without opening his eyes, Fred replied, "Yeah, there's supposed to be a medical kit under the seat of each vehicle. Some should be in there."

"Well, I'm leaving," Ches announced. "Will you two be okay?" he asked Trey and Diana.

"Yeah, we're gonna' get these two to the hospital; then, we'll try and locate you," Trey replied. Standing, he stuck his hand out. "You, go get em'."

"No hug?" Ches asked.

Gripping Ches's hand, Trey replied, "Nah. I have Diana to hug now."

"Oh," Ches remarked. "Well, in that case, I'm off."

Trey suddenly became serious. "Hey, now you make sure you come back. I don't know what I'd do without you."

There was no response as Ches quickly transformed and took off in the direction of Brant, and Lana's scent.

**Evan** continued to glance over at Lana, who was in her black widow form running along-side him. He was angry she hadn't listened to him and had insisted on coming along with him and Jacob.

"No!" He had shaken his head. "You can't come with us."

Crossing her arms and turning her back to him, she refused to listen to anything he said. "I can help," she stated. "And, besides that, he's my brother."

"Lana—" Turning her toward him, Evan looked into her big brown eyes. "You have to do this for me. Go back to the cabin and wait for me there. And, take Diana with you."

Her gaze narrowed and she remained quiet for a brief moment.

He thought she might attempt to use her powers of persuasion on him. Then, she responded, "No, Evan. We're a couple now—man and wife. And, that means till death do us part."

His hands slipped from her shoulders. There was no reasoning with her. Not only would she be in danger; but, their child would be also.

Yes, he knew about the baby and his heart ached to tell her. However, he didn't want to tell her here and now, not in the middle of the forest, surrounded by death and destruction and heading into more danger. It should be in private, when they were alone and could celebrate together.

He himself hadn't known about it until he had transformed after escaping the van. His senses had been magnified due to the extreme danger; and then, when he smelled her blood, it was different—fresher, softer—like the feeling you have after taking a bath.

His tone was set. "If you won't listen to me, then stay close to me. And, if things become too dangerous, you get away as fast as you can."

"I won't leave you," she stated.

"Yes, you will." His brow creased as he was becoming somewhat irate. "Lana, you have to listen to me, just this once. Please." Slipping his arms around her, he pulled her toward him. His warm words wafted through her hair and into her ear. "I love you. I could never bear to see anything happen to you. So, please, promise me."

"All right, I promise," she lowly spoke as she pulled away and gently kissed his cheek. "I'll be careful."

His gaze narrowed as he suspiciously observed her. Her reply was too quick. Then, turning away from her, he quickly transformed. She and Jacob did the same.

# Chapter 19

**Brant** was spread across eighteen acres of land, tucked between the mountains and surrounded by heavy security fences equipped with a highly developed security system. It was obscured from ground level; however, could be seen by aerial view.

Jacob, Evan and Lana were approaching the compound from the rear, a mountainous area inaccessible to any normal human. They could observe the entire compound from where they were—about 100 feet from the nearest fence.

Suddenly, Jacob slammed to a screeching halt. Evan had to do double-time not to ram into the back of him. He was a massive black widow, a dark marble statue, acutely evaluating his surroundings. Then, quickly transforming, he ducked within the mouth of a large crevice of the mountain. Evan and Lana did the same.

"What'd we stop for?" Evan asked as he took Lana's hand.

Pointing to the fence surrounding Brant, Jacob noted, "The security system will pick up anything on the ground within fifty feet of it. His dark stare cut to Evan. "So, we have to get in the air to clear it."

Evan just nodded his head. Then, he turned

to Lana. "This is as far as you go. Okay?"

Her wide eyes portrayed the apprehension she felt; however, she slowly nodded her head.

"Thank you." Evan kissed her forehead and left her side to stand beside Jacob who was stationed at the entrance of the small cave.

"They have the building surrounded," Jacob lowly noted.

Evan's dark gaze shot to where the two sharp-shooters were, then passed over each man like a teacher who's on a fieldtrip counting the head of every child. There were thirty men in all.

"I have thirty gunmen," Evan affirmed as he searched Jacob's coal black eyes for any indication Jacob was worried or concerned, possibly confident, or just plain scared shitless. Nothing. Evan could sense nothing in the emotionless murky pits. He briefly wondered how Lucinda could stand that, looking into those two dark, emotionless spheres every day. She had to be some kind of woman. Jacob was lucky to have her.

Evan averted his attention back to the situation at hand and asked, "So, how many can you take?"

"Possibly half," Jacob replied. "The element of surprise is gone; and, they've gotten what they wanted—our coming to them." He then fell silent. For Evan, the guy's silence was like trying to see through mud.

A round moment passed, then Jacob finally spoke. His tone was glum. "This is going to be a bloodbath. The survival rate will be low."

The words were chilling enough to make a

normal human balk; however, Evan had been down this road before and knew the risks. His question brought the minutest of reactions to Jacob's iron stare.

"Are you ready to die?"

"No, not yet," Jacob responded flatly. "Just repulsed sometimes by those who are living."

Evan nodded his head slowly. Being hunted and having to hide all those years had taken its toll at times. However, he wasn't ready to die yet either; he now had Lana and a child to look forward to. His heart soared at the thought, nearly ached at the giddiness that accompanied the idea of him not only being a husband, but, a father now too.

"Well, let's do this," Evan stated with finality.

Jacob raised one dark brow. "You do realize you could be killed."

"Well..." Evan said as he began to transform, "...It'll save you from bloodying your hands."

Jacob's eyes narrowed to slits.

Suddenly, Evan became tense, battle ready. Immediately, he maneuvered himself between the cave opening and Lana.

Ches appeared from out of nowhere.

"What are you doing here?" Evan angrily hissed, his black iris voodoo blazing with fury.

Quickly transforming and wrapping himself with his webbing, Ches answered, "I'm here to protect Lana."

"She doesn't need your help." Evan's shoulders quivered with rage as he fought to maintain control.

Ches stepped forward and lightly placed a hand on Lana's shoulder. "Well, I think she does."

Quick as lightning, Evan shoved Ches away. "Get your hands off her!"

Growling, Jacob grabbed Evan. "Knock it off!" Then, he angrily pointed at him, his face a mask of disgust. "You need to get your act together. And, you..." his finger angrily shot in Ches's direction. "...You need to back off! If you two want to kill each other after today, that's fine with me. However, right now, you are on my time, and I will not tolerate this nonsense."

"Evan, please..." Lana stated as she hugged herself. A chill ran along her spine as the memory of her parent's death was flooding her mind. "Let's just get Samuel and get out of here."

He could see the warranted pain in her eyes; it matched the quiver in her voice. Horrific memories were beginning to creep into his mind also. His chest was becoming tight.

"All right," he stated with finality.

"Good," Jacob's tone was set as he again pointed to Ches. "You stay here with Lana."

"No!" Evan seethed through clenched teeth. "He's not staying with her."

Jacob spun and grabbed Evan's face in a vice-like grip. "I'm sick of this!" he growled.

Lana hurriedly stepped between them. "No!" she cried as she, instinctively, attempted to use her eye control on Jacob. However, in the blink of an eye, Jacob had her clutched around the throat.

"Don't you ever try and control me," he spewed into her face, the male black widow surging inside him.

Evan immediately lunged at Jacob. "Don't you dare touch her, Jacob!"

## Brant

**"Sergeant,** can you still see the subjects?" Doctor Leanette Horn narrowed her cat-like eyes as she stared out the window on the heavy metal door and her cold hands wrung like the rollers on a press.

"Yes, ma'am." The sergeant's left hand slid to the firearm at his side while his eyes were glued to the binoculars pressed to the bridge of his nose. "The men are in place."

"Good," she replied, a mild sadistic pleasure seeping through her voice. "I knew they would eventually come; it was just a matter of time."

"Yes, ma'am, you were right." Lowering the binoculars, he removed the wooden toothpick from the corner of his mouth. "We'll take care of them."

"Oh, I know you will," she replied siltily. "That's your job."

His large frame shifted as he looked into her stone-like face. He had just been promoted due to the fact that the higher ranking officers had been unaccounted for, possibly even killed during their mission to retrieve the subjects. However, this doctor's position at Brant afforded her the luxury of being vicious to whomever she felt. She was a witch, a broom Hilda who had him by the throat; and, she was digging her scarlet nails in deep, threatening to pierce the surface of his skin.

Growling beneath his breath, he spun on his booted heels, and headed toward the door on the opposite end of the room. He'd be sure to make adequate distance between himself and the miserable hag, though China would still be too close. And, she certainly shouldn't be driving an Audi, he thought. Her style was more like push broom or just plain old Rubbermaid.

Chuckling at his own joke, he yanked the heavy door open and stepped out into the corridor. The men were in position, covering the entire perimeter of the base by either sharp shooter or ready armed man.

"I always thought that witches got along with spiders." His lone voice, along with the clicking of his heels, echoed off the stark white walls; while the buzzing of the overhead fluorescent lights was just another annoyance. Grabbing the handle to the exit door, he blinked at the terse sunlight that bit at his eyes.

"Shit, it's too nice out to be doing this today. I should be home playing foosball with the boy." Removing his walkie-talkie from his holster, he pressed the button then spoke, "Men—on my command."

"Roger that," the various voices proclaimed in unison.

Suddenly, he noticed the background noise. It reminded him of the ruckus his teenage daughter called rock and roll which blared from her stereo after school. However, it wasn't a melody or anything composed of musical notes; it was something else, it was the screeching raucous of arachnid beasts.

Repressing the button, he relayed another command. "Oh, and, someone see about getting those other half-baked beasts inside under control, sedate them or something."

"What—the doctors?" One of his men chided.

The captain chuckled along with the several snickers coming from the small speaker. "No, wise ass—the spiders inside there. They're causing a helluva ruckus."

Sliding the two-way radio back into its leather holster, he pulled his firearm from his side and clicked off the safety. Something told him this wouldn't be a walk in the park.

# Chapter 20

**Jacob** tossed Lana to the side like a rag doll and, within seconds, was transformed into his arachnid beast. Evan transformed also. The fight was instant, vicious, a battle to the end.

Suddenly, a shot rang out and Jacob dropped to the ground. Evan spun to help protect Lana; however, Ches was already in his arachnid form shielding her. He was a massive wall of protection against the swarm of bullets which were trapping them within the small cave.

Struggling against the conflicted emotions, he would either control, or allow to swallow him, Evan turned and charged out the cave's mouth, down the mountain and toward the military compound.

**Evan** pressed onward trying to avoid the onslaught of bullets racing toward him.

He was certain that after their fight, Jacob would have gone home—force him, Lana and Ches to handle the situation on their own. However, Jacob was, surprisingly, still an ally, just thirty feet away and flanking Evan's right side.

Suddenly, Evan buckled as one of his eight legs was hit and he staggered to the ground.

Come on! His human mind roared as Lana's face appeared before him and the sound of his child's tiny heartbeat, which he had heard earlier, sang in his ears.

The safety of his new family would depend on his and Jacob's success today. It was the driving force that would prevent him from giving up when the odds were so terribly against him.

He was headed toward the main building and was close enough to hear the cartridge clips being slid into their rifles as the sharp shooters readied their weapons.

Concentrating on the clicking of steel, he shot webbing from his spinnerets in that direction.

Several men scattered in the attempt to escape the sticky strands that raced to encase their bodies. Within seconds, he had taken out seven, while Jacob was still on the move.

"Men, hold steady!" The shout boomed amongst the thoop of discharged ammo and the cries from injured soldiers. During the onslaught, Evan suddenly paused; his fangs were clamped onto someone's neck; however, he listened closely.

It was the sound of other arachnids. Their shrieks were wild and unruly and their smell filtered through the thick of blood and into his pumping nostrils. The military base was apparently full of their kind, undomesticated humans who had mutated to black widow spiders and were ignited by the upheaval and presence of him and Jacob.

They were trying to escape, trying to break

free from captivity. Some of these black widows had been incarcerated for years, never free to the outside world and never to live as civilized people.

Evan briefly wondered if Samuel was among them.

Freeing them was asking for trouble, especially if any of them were unruly males. His body stiffened at the knowledge that there definitely were several.

Lana... His mind galloped through the perilous damage that could be done since Ches would never be able to hold off a horde of male arachnid beasts.

What had they gotten themselves into?

Ripping his fangs free from the dangling corpse before him, he abruptly spun and began to make his way back to where Lana and Ches were. However, he was suddenly struck by two bullets that tore through his exoskeleton and sent him head first to the ground.

**Thunder** filled the air and the earth shook beneath Evan. It was the compound's west wall crashing open as huge, monstrous arachnids, climbing through the dust and rubble, emerged as gargantuan uncontrollable beasts—beasts which were hungry.

Shit! Evan groaned. Stumbling forward, he hurried away from the carnage that was befalling all those who were human and all those who were smaller, more timid arachnids. It was survival of the fittest.

Evan's beast called out to Lana warning her

of the impending danger. Hopefully, she would understand, get away before it was too late.

Two massive arachnid males suddenly trampled Evan in their determined plight to reach Lana first. Oh my god! He wanted to scream—shout to her and Ches who he could see in the far off distance.

Ches was transformed, positioned on the side of the mountain between the two males and Lana. He was ready to fight. However, Lana stood frozen; the terror emanating from her was like a bouquet of wine, while the male arachnids were the drunks.

The two males hit Ches with the force of a train. Evan watched as Ches was thrown backward and fought to regain his footing and keep from being bludgeoned to death.

Evan's gaze froze on Lana and he raced across the terrain to where she was. She was trying to transform as one of the males attacked her. He had her belly-down so she was unable to use the power in her eyes.

Laaaaannnnaaa!!!! He propelled himself forward, ramming headfirst into the huge beast and sending him stumbling backward.

Quickly, the huge arachnid leapt to its feet and charged Evan. The ripping and tearing, and gnashing of teeth filled the air as another male joined the fight. Suddenly, there were two more, then two more. Evan and Ches were outnumbered.

Evan fought with a vengeance knowing Lana and the baby's life depended on him. No matter what, he wouldn't let them die.

Run, Lana! he shouted inside. Run—get away!

Suddenly, two more black widows joined the fight. One was male, the other female. Surprisingly, they fought alongside him and Ches, fought to fend-off the beasts that were now raging at them in numbers.

Could one of them be Samuel? Evan thought as he struggled to remain positioned between the other arachnids and Lana.

Evan's strength was waning and his injuries were deep. For him, the fighting seemed an eternity as one beast after another attacked them. And, though the tiniest heartbeat he had previously heard beat no longer and his heart ached at the loss, he was determined to protect her.

The monster paid; Evan ripped him to shreds.

**After** what seemed hours, the fighting stopped and the beasts scattered.

Lana lay unconscious on the ground. Hurriedly transforming, Evan raced to her side.

"Lana?" He gently took her into his arms.

"Is she okay," the arachnid that had been fighting alongside him asked after transforming. He was a young blonde-haired, green-eyed boy. Evan thought it might be Samuel by the similarity in the boy's and Lana's blood; however, he maintained his guard.

"Are you Samuel?" Evan hurriedly asked.

"Yeah, I'm her brother."

Samuel touched Lana's shoulder. "Lana?

Lana!" He then turned to Evan. "Is she going to be okay?"

Brushing the wild strands of hair from Lana's face, Evan lightly stroked her cheek. "I think so—I hope so." He called to her, "Lana..."

Slowly, her eyes blinked as she winced in pain and, immediately, clutched at her stomach.

"Ow, something's not right."

"You were hit pretty hard." He attempted a smile though his heart was breaking at the loss of their child and he didn't want to tell her. "Oh, and, look who's here to see you." Evan shifted his weight to give her a full view of Samuel.

She blinked her eyes again; her words were just a whisper. "Samuel? Is that really you?" Achingly, she reached for him and pulled him toward her; tears poured along her trembling cheeks.

"Yeah," he barely choked the words as he clung to her tightly and began to cry. "I was so worried about you."

Jacob approached the three. "Well, it is finished. There are no human survivors." His cold stare then locked with Evan's.

"And, Evan Labonte, this had best be the last time I ever see you. For, the next time, I may just kill you." With that, he turned and transformed on the move as he cleared the opening in the cave and headed toward home.

# Chapter 21

## Heaven

**Ches** lay on the ground in his human form, his body badly injured and each breath a labored task. His eyes searched the large sky, staring into the cerulean blue vastness, searching for an answer as to why his life had taken such a turn.

A massive shadow inked its way between him and the bright light overhead. Ches blinked his eyes at what he saw.

It was a small black widow female who stared down at him with eight, large, curious eyes. Her scent was like heaven, the most wonderful bouquet he'd ever had the pleasure of inhaling. And, the aura emanating from her was incredulous, like the cool water of a crystal clear pond on a hot summer's day.

Was he in Heaven? Had he died while trying to protect Lana?

His voice croaked like a frog as he spoke. "Am I dead?"

The female black widow cocked her head to the side slightly as if amazed he could speak.

"I guess you can't understand me." Groaning, he sat up. And, running a hand through his mop of disheveled hair, he glanced around trying to recall what had happened.

No. He wasn't in heaven. Heaven wouldn't have the smell of dead human and arachnid bodies soaking the air. And, pain wasn't supposed to be there either.

Maybe this was hell, he thought as he placed his hand over the gash on his arm. No, he answered himself with the one syllable word for the second time; hell wouldn't have such an alluring creature like the one he had standing before him in it.

What was going on? And, where were Evan and Lana?

The female black widow's shadow shifted as she quietly moved to stand behind him. For some strange reason, his senses approved of her presence, allowed her to position herself behind him where he would be most vulnerable to an attack by her. She was transforming into her human state. Ches slowly turned around, his gaze focusing on her from the knees down.

"Are you okay?" Her voice was soft as an angel's wings.

"Yeah," he quietly replied. "Were you the one helping us?"

"Yes," she responded.

"Where are the others, Evan and Lana?"

"They're just over the knoll between the rocks. Samuel is with them."

Ches looked up into her face. She looked to be about eighteen; and, for a brief moment, he was stunned at how lovely she was. "Did you say, 'Samuel'?"

"Yes, I did," she softly answered. "He and I were held on the same block in Brant."

She extended a slender hand before her. "My name is Heather."

## Four Weeks Later

**Evan** switched the key off on the motorcycle; and, removing his hat, he brushed a hand through the hair pasted to his head. Lana swore he'd lose his hat if he wore it while riding; he was determined he wouldn't.

Lana was presently at the cabin sleeping. She had been devastated to know she had lost their child during the massacre and had wept day and night, awakening Evan from his sleep as she'd quietly cry out and awake to a tear-stained pillow. However, Samuel's presence had helped tremendously and the joy of her brother being returned safely to her had somewhat helped to alleviate her sadness about the baby.

Evan had insisted that they wait a bit before trying to conceive again. However, Lana was persistent, desiring to give Evan that which he never had—a large family, and to compensate somewhat for the loss of her and Samuel's parents. So, now she was at home sleeping, her belly the size of a small cantaloupe and the cabin looking like the entire newborn section from Babies "R" Us.

Evan couldn't help but beam inside. They were having a girl: He could tell by the scent of Lana's blood. And each time he laid his head to Lana's stomach and listened to the tiny thump,

thump, thump of his unborn daughter's heartbeat, tears of joy stung at the back of his eyes and he loved them both even more.

Of course, Lana was concerned with her pregnancy and the delivery of the baby. She worried about it day and night  and probably would until the delivery.

"I won't hurt the baby, will I?" she had asked Evan on multiple occasions. Worry plagued her large dark eyes. "You have to promise me that you'll be here for the delivery; and, under no circumstance can you leave me alone then."

"I promise," he stated gently as he held her hand and laid his head for the hundredth time on her belly.

He would never be separated from his two girls.


**Climbing** from the bike, Evan and Samuel headed toward Jacob and Lucinda's cottage. It was odd how he and Samuel had immediately hit it off, especially since they were both male arachnids. In fact, Evan loved Samuel, loved him like a younger brother.

It was fun to take Samuel riding, take him at high speeds through the back roads while showing off with a wheelie or two. Neither could be killed, so why not push the bike to its limit, see what power they had between their legs. Of course, Lana would be furious if she found out; but, who was telling. And, one day he would have to get Samuel his own bike, possibly a canary yellow one.

Horsing around at the cabin with Samuel was great fun too. However, the cabin roof was taking a real beating—taking a beating from being used as a spring board by their arachnid beasts. Lana insisted it would stop when the baby came; and, Evan restrained from horsing around when she was resting. So, on those days, he and Samuel went out on the bike or worked on something outside.

Evan's attention was drawn to the cottage as Lucinda stepped out onto the porch. Apparently, she had gone against Jacob's wishes, which she never did, and had called Evan and asked him to come out. She said that Jacob needed his help.

Evan hadn't spoken to Jacob since the day they retrieved Samuel from Brant which was several weeks ago. Miraculously, he, Ches and Jacob were able to ward off the vast amount of wild and unruly arachnids that had escaped the facility that day, then scattered like a pack of rats. Eventually, the other arachnids would resurface and have to be dealt with. Evan hoped that wasn't the situation today.

He was closer to the house now and his gaze settled on Lucinda's large green eyes. Fear overshadowed their emerald glow.

"Lucinda—is everything okay?" Calling to her, he quickened his steps.

Her hand quickly slipped to her apron pocket where she removed a small slip of lilac colored paper which was folded several times and had the single word "Mommy" written on the outer fold. Trembling slightly, she handed it to Evan.

"I found this in the twin's room."
Hurriedly, Evan opened the note and read it.

Dear Mommy,

We know Daddy was leving to hunt the spiders. We wanted to go two. But, you would say no. So, we already went ahead. You are probbably mad at us. Don't worry we can take care of our selfs. Aimery gets as big as a house when he transsforms and I am faster than Uncle Evan's motor bike when I turn into a spider. It is realy cool. I made sure to pack a drink and a snack in each of our back packs. I gave Aimery 2. You know how hungry he gets. We love you and took some change from the kictchen jar before we left so we could call you. We will pay it back when we get home.

Love   Aimery and Aimee

**Slowly** folding the paper, Evan gently placed it in Lucinda's hand.

There was so much territory to cover; but, they would be found. However, he wouldn't be able to do this on his own; he needed a minute to sort out their options.

Well, there was Jacob, Lucinda, Lana, Samuel, Heather, he mentally calculated the number of allied arachnids he knew that could be counted on. Oh, and also Ches. Blah, the guy's name made the lunch he had earlier taste sour.

Well, Lana was with child. She certainly couldn't go. And, with Lucinda's aging at every transformation, she would be like molded bread by the time they returned from locating the children.

Well, he could definitely count on Samuel; Samuel was rad as a black widow, fast and powerful, definitely a worthy ally.

That left Jacob and...Ches. Evan cringed at the thought. Why did just the mention of Ches's name rub him the wrong way? Though it was somewhat better between the two of them since Heather had come into the picture; and, for the briefest of milliseconds, he had appreciated the guy's presence during their fight at Brant, he still owed the guy a good kick in the ass.

Maybe he would have his chance if they were out this time together, alone, without either of the girls coming between their fighting, which they always did.

Maybe he could really get Ches alone this time and kick his sorry butt good.

An odd smile crept upon his lips and Lucinda glanced at him strangely.

Quickly hugging her, he stated, "Don't worry, Lucinda. We'll bring them back."

"No, you won't," Jacob's voice came from inside the screen door. He stepped out onto the porch. "I'll handle this."

His disapproving stare cut to Lucinda, then to Evan, and lastly to Samuel who had remained with the bike.

"Lucinda had no right to call you; this is a family affair... So, leave."

"But, Jacob..." Lucinda's voice quavered as his hand shot to the air, a sign for her to be silent.

Her tired eyes looked to Evan in apology.

Evan's brows creased. "I'm not doing this for you, Jacob. I'm doing this for Aimery and Aimee." He added, "And, of course, for Lucinda."

Jacob's fangs suddenly appeared and he hissed.

"I said, 'no'. And, you brought another arachnid male here: Lucinda is with child. I should kill you both."

"You could try, Jacob," Evan snarled.

"Jacob, please." Lucinda gently touched his arm. Her green eyes swam with large droplets which would soon fall upon her etched cheeks.

Jacob's icy stare cut to Lucinda's face, then to her large belly. He was silent for a moment and then spoke.

"My apologies to you and our unborn child. However..." His narrowed gaze shot to Evan. "If we cross paths again, Evan Labonte, I will be sure to make it our last. This time I promise."

Then, turning to Lucinda he stated, "I'm leaving now. I will call you with any news." Kissing her cheek, he disappeared inside the house and out of sight.

"Evan..." Lucinda began, "...I'm so sorry..."

Evan quickly stepped forward. "No, no. It's

okay. I'm the one who owes you the apology. I shouldn't have brought Samuel here. And, it was rude of me to even think of fighting in your presence."

Lucinda's hand gently went to his cheek. "Oh, Evan, you have been such a blessing in our lives. You never need to apologize to me."

Smiling warmly, she softly embraced him. "Also, I would like to come and visit with Lana soon. Would that be okay?"

"Of course," he responded as he stepped away. "You and the twins are welcome anytime. Well, we have to get going. Goodbye, Lucinda. We'll do what we can."

Evan turned on his heels and descended the steps two at a time.

"Whadrya gonna' do, Evan?" Samuel asked as Evan approached. He had been able to hear everything.

"I'm gonna' call Ches, maybe see if he'll go along with us."

Samuel frowned. "I thought you hated Ches."

"Just about every minute of the day," Evan answered sourly. "But, I still owe the guy, so I figure this will be my chance to repay him."

"Repay him for what?" Samuel's wide eyes gleamed with curiosity.

Evan thought about that for a moment, then he answered. "For just being annoying."

"Oh," Samuel's gaze dropped along with his shoulders. He was itching for something interesting, something besides the fact that Ches loved Lana. That's usually what Evan griped about all day long. That was becoming annoying.

Evan jimmied his cell phone from his pocket.

With Lana being pregnant, she had insisted that Ches's cell phone number be on speed dial in both she and Evan's phones.

Ches loved Heather—loved her with all his heart. However, he still cared for Lana; and, Evan hated it.

Evan pushed the numeral "0" on his cell phone for nothing, zero, big fat loser. Then, placing his hat on his head, he waited for Ches to answer the phone.

"Hello?"

"Ches...buddy..." Evan smiled wickedly as the image of Ches with a purple eye and bloody nose entered his mind.

"Whaddaya want, Evan?"

Evan continued to grin. "Hey, two of our kind are in trouble. I'm gonna' need your help."

Samuel just laughed.

Suddenly, the call alert on Evan's phone flashed blue. It was a text message from Lana. Evan quickly scanned it, then his gaze raced to the bike.

"What is it?" Samuel asked.

"We have to go," Evan anxiously answered as he flipped his cell phone closed and hung up on Ches. "The baby's coming!"

LOOK FOR TESSA LAROCK'S
NEW TITLES TO COME:

### For Teens:
Evil Be Thy Name

### Children's Books:
Rosette and the Golden Egg

And, many more...

Breinigsville, PA USA
16 July 2010
241912BV00001B/5/P